Undeath and the Detective

NINE SPOOKY MYSTERIES

Edited by
Jess Faraday

Contributions by
Helen Angove, Leonard August, Emily Baird
H. Tucker Cobey, Charlie Cochrane, Lynn Finger
Mark Hague, Gay Toltl Kinman, Angelia Sparrow

Cover Art by
Virginia Cantarella

ELM BOOKS, 2013
Laramie, Wyoming

Undeath and the Detective edited by Jess Faraday
Copyright © 2013 by Elm Books
Paperback ISBN: 978-0-9886116-7-2
E-Format ISBN: 978-0-9886116-6-5
Print Edition

Elm Books
1175 State Highway 130
Laramie, WY 82070
(http://elm-books.com)

Cover illustration by Virginia Cantarella
(http://www.virginiacantarella.com)

Copy editing by M.M. Ardagna

Formatting by BB eBooks
(http://bbebooksthailand.com)

Typeface: Cochin

CONTENTS

FOREWORD

WHEN I WAS putting together our second anthology, *Death and the Detective*, I was looking for a very specific category of mystery—a category that excluded supernatural stories. However, stating as much in the submission call had exactly the opposite effect. Within a few days of posting the call, I began to receive nothing *but* supernatural stories, with plaintive cover letters urging me to make an exception *just this once*. I joked to the publisher, Leila Monaghan, that we should do a Halloween anthology of all supernatural mysteries. We could call it *Undeath and the Detective*.

Leila thought that was a very good idea.

It also turned out to be enormous fun.

The stories in *Undeath and the Detective* will take you from the Age of Sail—the early 1800s—to the distant future, and many places between. You'll meet ghosts—spectral and technological; zombies, little green men, and yes, even the occasional shifter and vamp. You'll come up against philosophical questions such as *What is the price of achieving your dreams?* and *Is it murder if the victim is already dead?* You'll meet a few well-known authors, be reunited with some of your Elm Books favorites, and discover some talented newcomers.

But most importantly, I hope you'll enjoy the stories as much as I have.

Jess Faraday
October 2013

SECRETS

by
Charlie Cochrane

1804
Aboard the frigate Hecuba, two bells in the last dog watch.

ONLY A FOOL would barge into Stephen Hopkins's great cabin unannounced, especially when he was in conference with his first Lieutenant. So when Midshipman Rogerson burst through the door, he got the reception he deserved. "Are we beating to quarters?" Captain Hopkins demanded, dark eyes glowering below a mass of dark hair, which seemed reluctant to stay tied back.

"No, sir." Rogerson was a sensible lad of fifteen, two years now at sea and utterly absorbed with serving King and country, so why he'd taken such leave of his senses as to come in unannounced was an utter mystery.

"Then, Mr. Rogerson, you are forgetting yourself. What is the meaning of this?" The lantern shadows on the captain's face gave it an unnaturally solemn appearance. Barely more than ten years older than the midshipman, but with all those years' experience in his pocket, Hopkins seated at his own table in his own well-furnished cabin was a formidable man.

"It's a monster, sir. Two points off the larboard beam and very close. Mr. Douglas said you were to be notified immediately, sir." Rogerson was usually a bundle of nerves when in the presence of his superior officers, but on this occasion he was strangely animated.

First Lieutenant Simon Paget smiled. Despite being the same age as the captain, he gave the illusion of being younger, less careworn, if no less a sailor. "I've always heard about other people seeing sea serpents but I never

2

believed it could be true. You're not attempting to fool us, are you?"

The young man looked horrified. "Of course not, sir. It's there all right, come and see."

Lieutenant Paget caught Hopkins's eye and managed by another smile to defuse the anger brewing there. He picked up his hat and placed it over his tawny, short cut locks. "There's not a moment to lose, Captain."

The scene on deck was like a tableau. From Douglas, the ship's master, down to the meanest foremast jack, men were frozen in their places, eyes fixed on the object in the water. The sun had set early, it being only weeks from the shortest day, but the steady stream of moonlight made observation easy—this was no optical illusion. This was indeed a monster: huge, menacing, and slowly approaching the frigate.

A long neck rose from the water like a sinuous mast, with a head that seemed too small to grace the body carrying it. That body could be seen just breaking the water—a massive bulk, as big as a finner—shining sleekly. There was the impression of a long, strong tail following behind, making Douglas mumble about Behemoth and whether this beast also ate grass like the ox, or if its preferred food was jack tars.

"Ye Gods," Hopkins muttered and gripped the rail.

Even Paget was speechless; his boyish enthusiasm had disappeared at the terror which permeated the crew. The beast made several more passes of the ship—very close this time, its foul breath flooding the air—and then was gone, diving like a dolphin into the waves and creating a swell which rocked Hecuba like a toy.

BACK IN THE GREAT CABIN, Hopkins took the whisky bottle in unsteady hands and poured himself a stiff shot, then another for Paget, and finally one for Douglas. "We had a bit of a fright there, gentlemen. Need to get the three of us revived."

Paget accepted the drink gratefully. It barely touched the sides making its way down, and it hardly touched the chill he felt. "What was it, Mr. Hopkins? I've heard people talk about monsters—giant squid and sea dragons—but I never believed I'd see one."

"Admiral Cornwallis had a sea monster from the West Indies. A Jenny Haniver they call them," Douglas chipped in. "Ugly looking thing, like a devil."

Hopkins snorted. "I've seen many of those and I've seen men making them, too. The dried skeleton of a ray, all twisted up so that the nostrils look like eyes."

"Yet people fall for them," Paget said, shaking his head at such stupidity. "Although what we saw wasn't anything man-made. It breathed. And you could hear it and smell it, couldn't you, Mr. Douglas?"

"Indeed, sir. In all my years at sea, I've never come across the like. We used to hear the odd tale back home about lake horses, but I'd no idea they were any more than the result of overindulgence in the water of life." Douglas lifted his glass. "I never thought I'd need the same stuff to revive me after I'd seen one."

"Will you mention it in the log, sir? The afternoon we almost got boarded by a sea serpent?" Paget managed one of his usual jokes, even though his heart wasn't in it—this thing had shaken him.

"I will enter as good a description as we can muster, but I wish we had a naturalist aboard to help me."

"Young Thompson could oblige, sir." The master nodded then finished his dram. "He knows all his birds and fish. I assume he wouldn't have missed the chance to see the thing."

"Fetch him, please, Mr. Douglas. We can set to while things are fresh in our minds."

"Fresh in our minds?" Paget said, once they were alone. "I can't imagine I will ever forget that sight."

Hopkins shivered. "Aye. It turned my blood cold, too."

Paget leaned closer, hand just grazing his captain's. "Then I feel it my bounden duty to offer to warm it once more. I know an excellent method. Or two."

"Hush," Hopkins replied with a grin. "Keep that service 'til later. In the meantime help me find the right words to put in the log."

The drafting and re-drafting was interrupted by Rogerson, knocking first, this time, before making a more restrained entrance.

"Please, Captain Hopkins, sir, Mr. Douglas says could you come?"

"Is the monster back again?" Hopkins's voice suggested this was a prospect he didn't relish.

"No, sir." The midshipman's earlier excitement had gone; now he looked terrified.

"What is it, then?" Paget spoke kindly.

"It's Thompson, sir. He's disappeared."

THEY FOUND DOUGLAS at the entrance to the middies'
mess, the air full of the odor of unwashed young men,
something far worse than the sea serpent's breath. He'd
already organized a search of the vessel, especially
Thompson's favorite corners—places where he would go
when off watch to study beetles or read. Hopkins nodded
his approval of all they'd done; there were only so many
places on a ship where the boy could have gone. The
thought of him not actually being on board any more
wasn't one to contemplate just yet.

"Mr. Rogerson." Paget drew the lad quietly aside. "Is
there anybody distressing Mr. Thompson? I know the
middies' mess isn't always a friendly place." He vividly
recalled the difficulties of being that age. Fourteen was
neither childhood nor manhood.

Rogerson looked blank. "Nobody was bothering
Thompson, sir. He never lets anything get to him."

A muffled shout of protest indicated something was
getting to Thompson now—two burly tars. Both the
seamen towered above the midshipman, a head taller at
least, but he seemed to be making a rare fist of trying to
get out of their iron grips as they dragged him up the
ladder and into the lantern's glare.

"Found him, sir." The sailors addressed the captain,
saluted, and looked scared. Thompson—a perky-looking
lad cursed with an expansive crop of freckles—seemed
unaware of the upheaval he'd caused.

"Where have you been, Mr. Thompson?" Hopkins's
eyes narrowed.

"In the cable tiers, sir." The young midshipman answered, confidently.

"And what were you doing there?"

"Oh, I was talking to the White Admiral, sir."

"Who?" All three officers' voices joined in a single note.

"The White Admiral, sir. He's not one of the crew, or anything. I suppose you'd call him a spirit."

No wonder the men who'd found him looked nervous.

"He's a pleasant old cove, you know," Thompson blethered on, seemingly unaware of the sensation he was creating. "He always has a word in season as they say," the young man added, as if it were the most natural thing in the world to converse with ghosts.

"Always?" Paget echoed. "Have you met him before?"

"Oh yes, sir. He appears quite regularly and wants to have a chat."

Hopkins gave his lieutenant a look, which shouted, 'The boy's gone mad,' but Paget just shrugged.

Douglas recovered his tongue first. He'd often said he'd heard Drake's Drum at the battle of Cape St. Vincent and understood the effect of the supernatural on sailors. "Are you sure this isn't just one of the foremast jacks playing a trick on you? I've known all sorts of dodges to be played on midshipmen."

"Oh no, Mr. Douglas. It wasn't like the time I was sent to ask for a 'long weight.' No foremast jack could walk through a solid bulkhead like it was made of mist, could he?" That seemed conclusive, assuming it had happened. "He fought under the old Queen—Elizabeth the first I mean, begging your pardon—and what he says about the olden days rings true. Apparently he was a wicked old cove."

Paget couldn't help but see the ludicrous side of the situation. A ghost who dropped in for a friendly chat? "Wicked? What did he do?"

"Ah, he's never very clear about that. Something about being too pally with the Spanish. But his spirit has to stay here on earth until he's earned the right to enter his eternal rest. Leastways, that's what he says."

An insidious, cold atmosphere had spread through those present, much more rapidly than it had done at the sight of the monster. Sea serpents were one thing, but a ghost—a voluble, frequently appearing ghost—was quite another.

Hopkins looked bleak; this matter clearly bothered him even more than the beast had. "Are you saying—?" The captain's question was interrupted by the arrival of the lieutenant of marines, with two of his men in tow. "Yes, Henman?"

If everyone who'd heard Thompson's story of the admiral had turned pale, then Henman's face out-ashened them all.

"Could you come with us to the hold, sir? Now. It's important."

"I will." Hopkins passed a hand over his brow. "Mr. Douglas, can you make sure Thompson gets a hot meal inside him? Ask my steward to rouse out the last of the chicken broth. That'll settle him down for a reasonable night's sleep."

The looks on the faces of the rest of the midshipmen indicated Thompson might be the only one of them in that happy position. What if this White Admiral, whoever he was, might want to have a word in season with them?

"Mr. Paget?" Hopkins motioned for his first officer to join him as they followed the marines along the deck and down the nearest ladder. "What is it I'm being taken to see?" he asked, once they were out of earshot of the crew.

"A dead man. The surgeon's with him, but he's beyond even Mr. Cowan's care. Here." Henman pointed as they reached the hold. Two marines were standing watch, holding a lantern, while Cowan bent over a twisted body.

"Who is it?" Hopkins asked.

"Ponting," Cowan said, easing himself up off his haunches. "The side of his head's been stoved in. With this, I suspect." He pointed to a blood-smeared belaying pin, which Paget—gingerly—picked up and held at arm's length.

"When might this have happened?" the captain continued, eyeing the wooden pin with distaste.

"Sometime during the last couple of hours, I'd say. Perhaps when we were all busy looking at the beast." The surgeon wiped his hands on a towel.

"Not all of us. Two at least would have been here. But who'd have noticed who wasn't present when all eyes were on the monster?" Paget looked down at the body. Ponting had joined them at Portsmouth and had proved not a bad sailor, nor an unpopular man. "Why?"

"I can't divine that." Cowan smiled ruefully. "But if he could be moved into a better light he might tell me more."

"Make it so. And report to me as soon as you can. Gentlemen," Hopkins said, looking at each man in turn. "If anyone asks, you will say that Ponting has suffered an accident, is dangerously ill, and that the surgeon is treating him. Otherwise I would expect you to keep your eyes open and your mouths shut. You've been admirably discreet so far," he added, nodding his approval at the marines. "If you hear anything which might cast light on the matter, make me or Mr. Paget aware of it."

Cowan nodded, slowly and thoughtfully. "Will you tell the men the truth tomorrow?"

"I've not decided. Perhaps if whoever did this thinks Ponting is still alive he'll try again. It would be as well that perhaps one of your burliest men might have to be confined to sick bay for a few days, Mr. Henman."

"I'll ensure that happens," Henman replied with a grim smile.

"A monster, a ghost, and a murder," Paget said, airing all their thoughts. "Please God there'll be no more alarums tonight."

"DO YOU BELIEVE IN GHOSTS, SIMON?" Hopkins's hand had at last steadied itself enough to pour out another stiff measure of whisky for the both of them.

"Do you, Stephen?" The great cabin had always felt a place of retreat, of quiet calm, but now the brooding atmosphere had penetrated even here. Paget sat alongside his captain, by the great window. The night was dark, but the mood was darker. "It goes against my sense of logic, but what does one do when spirits raise themselves and come visiting on board, like some poor old yellow admiral from Plymouth paying us a social call?"

"This is no laughing matter." The captain shuddered, tossing back half his drink. "Thompson isn't the only one on this ship who sees ghosts."

"What do you mean?"

"Three times this last month I've thought I saw my father and he's been dead, what, near a twelvemonth, now?"

"Good God." Paget took a hefty swig of whisky. "Why didn't you tell me this before?" For a captain not to confide such a thing to a junior officer he could understand, but his relationship with Hopkins went beyond the ship. They might never show any hint of it aboard, but they'd been lovers these last three years— why hadn't Stephen mentioned these visitations?

"Because I thought I was going insane. No one else saw him, just me. And now this ship is beset with things I do not understand." Hopkins drained his drink, reached for the bottle, then pushed it away.

"When did this happen?"

"The first time was when we passed through that dense fog off Ushant. I thought I saw him pass across the quarterdeck. I decided it was merely my imagination— I'd not slept well and wasn't at my best."

Paget cradled the last of his whisky, trying to keep his wits about him. "But you saw him again?"

Hopkins nodded. "Once, he was up in the shrouds. The third time was..." He hesitated, then shivered. "The third time was here in the great cabin. I wonder... I wonder if he's unable to rest. If something ails his spirit."

"But he wasn't a wicked man, like Thompson's admiral confesses to have been."

"Not as long as I knew him, no. Although he'd been wild in his youth, before my mother tamed him, or so he said."

"Tomorrow we should head back to Plymouth and seek a priest." Paget raised his hand to stifle protest. "Let me speak. There's more than one spirit to deal with here. The men are already unsettled by this White Admiral — were they to get wind that another ghost walks abroad, they'd all be running once we hit the first friendly port."

"You're proposing an exorcism?"

"Of sorts. Perhaps he could lay troubled souls to rest, as well. It would certainly help to calm the men's minds." Paget rubbed his hands against the cold. "We'll ask for plenty of ceremony, incense and all. The men need the reassurance of seeing an outward manifestation of something happening, even if the priest speaks the actual service quietly, here in your cabin."

"And would your priest find a murderer?"

Well, there was the rub. "No. That's a matter for the secular authorities, not the spiritual."

"In that case, we don't touch land until we know who killed Ponting. Then you can have your exorcism, but not before." Hopkins's frown melted into a pale smile as he reached over and briefly caressed his first officer's hand. "I will not believe this ship is cursed. There'll be a prosaic explanation for everything. None the less grim for that, but prosaic."

"I wish I had your faith." Paget rose. Time to try to catch some sleep. He wasn't convinced their adventures were over.

"My faith? It's not big enough to warm your hands at."

"Then I'll have to be content with your trust." Paget's voice dropped to a whisper. Sentries might not be able to see through doors, but their hearing could be acute. "And the part of your heart I know is mine."

WHEN PAGET WOKE from dreams invaded by both Hamlet and Lear, Hopkins's words wouldn't shift from his mind.

The third time was here in the great cabin.

Why should Hopkins's father choose to haunt his son? He knew of no strain within the family—the two men had got along as well as father and son might, the only regret on Stephen's part being that his sire hadn't lived to see him made Captain.

A prosaic explanation for everything.

There could well be, for that element at least. Was Stephen conjuring up a vision of his much lamented father so he could show the man what a success he'd made of his career? And the sea monster could be easily explained, too. Perhaps these things were as real as sperm whales or giant squid, but modern naturalists had simply not yet captured a specimen to dissect, stuff, and display.

Which left the White Admiral, who might just be a figment of an overactive imagination—Paget remembered the tales he'd told his family and friends as a child and how he'd believed half of them—and a murdered man, who definitely wasn't anything but real. Maybe the surgeon would provide some much needed illumination.

But it soon became apparent—once Paget had joined Cowan, Douglas, and Hopkins in the great cabin for breakfast—that the surgeon had nothing new to add as far as the corpse was concerned. The only other marks it bore were evidence of a vicious flogging administered under a past captain. That was not of itself unusual, especially as Ponting had served with Hardy, a captain notorious for his love of the "cat."

"Did anybody try to visit him?" the captain asked, pouring himself a scalding hot coffee.

"Two of his messmates, who seemed genuinely concerned for the man's welfare," Cowan said. "I've treated him before, for a rotten tooth, and there were plenty of volunteers to look after him then. He always struck me as both civil and popular."

"But he was clearly unpopular with somebody." Hopkins sipped his coffee, mind clearly whirring as intently as if he were eyeing up a pair of French corvettes.

"I have a better idea of when he died," Cowan said, ladling sugar into his own cup. "His messmates said he'd been on deck with them when the monster was first sighted. He'd laughed and said they were imagining things. Then when it became clear there really was something to be seen, he said if they wanted to waste their time watching some toothless old whale that was up to them, but he had no interest in it. He went off about his business, although what that might have been they couldn't say. They weren't on watch."

"No," said Paget. "Douglas and I checked earlier. Are you confident he was killed while the creature was attempting to board us?"

"Mr. Paget, this is serious." Hopkins frowned disapproval at such levity.

"I know it is. I'm sorry, sir." Was there to be no more humor until this business was put to rest? As Ponting himself would soon have to be.

Cowan, at least, was smiling, if ruefully. "Although I can't be entirely sure, I believe that to be so. In which case, those of us who were watching it all the while — and that must have been a good twenty minutes or more — would not have been able to do the deed."

"Mr. Paget, will you arrange for each man to be asked about who he can account for during that time?"

"Yes, sir, if I can have Mr. Henman to help me or it'll take from here to kingdom come. And do I explain why I'm asking?" he added, aware that the news couldn't be kept from the crew for much longer. "If I tell them he's dead then your plan to flush out his killer will become redundant. But if I just say he's been attacked, they'll wonder why we're keeping him hidden."

"He'll make his presence known soon enough, especially in this heat," Cowan remarked drily.

Hopkins looked out of the window, maybe seeking inspiration from his beloved ocean. "Tell them he died in the night. That we believe he had an accident but can't be sure. That we hope somebody may have seen what happened to him."

"And if someone produces an elaborate tale of his falling down and striking his head on some sharp object, then presumably we have a trail to follow?" Paget nodded. "Yes, that might be the best strategy."

"Thompson wasn't on deck when we saw the monster," Douglas said quietly. "That's when the midshipmen first became concerned about him—they knew the lad would have loved to see such a thing."

Hopkins spun round. "Are you suggesting he had something to do with Ponting's death?"

"I am not, sir," Douglas bridled, as always protective of his brood of young gentlemen. Indeed, it seemed unlikely—Ponting was a handbreadth taller than Thompson, and twice the girth—but they couldn't discount it. The element of surprise and a convenient step or barrel could tip the odds. "But he may have seen someone else who did."

"I'll talk to him when I get round to the midshipmen," Paget said quickly. "He might be more forthcoming with me."

"Recognizes a fellow whippersnapper?" Hopkins hadn't entirely lost his sense of humor. "You're probably right. But you'll report what's said straight back to me."

"Of course. Word for word." Unless, perhaps, if it concerned any further ghostly apparitions.

PAGET, who'd questioned three dozen jacks without discovering anything other than that they'd all been gawping at the sea monster, even the ones who swore they were keeping a watch for French sails, decided it was time to tackle Thompson. He cut the lad out of his navigation lesson, for which he seemed more than grateful, not least because it made his fellow middies envious. They found a quiet corner—or what passed for one on a working ship.

"How are you feeling today?" Paget asked, in his most avuncular fashion.

"Cross, sir." Thompson replied, although his impish grin suggested anything but anger. "I missed seeing that sea monster. If only the White Admiral had been slightly earlier or later."

"Admirals always keep to their own plans, with no consideration of junior officers. You need to learn that." Paget grinned. "What was so important that he had to keep you from your beastie?"

"He was warning me, sir. He'd told me before that there was great evil aboard this ship but I didn't believe him. You and Captain Hopkins wouldn't stand for that, would you?"

"Not if we could help it, no." Paget tried to look cheerful despite the cold dart shooting up his spine.

"This time, he said that something had to be done. That he'd been sent to warn us." The impish grin was fading, and seemingly not just at the thought of having to return to his sines and cosines.

"Was that all? He didn't tell you the nature of this evil?"

"No, sir. There was a lot of stuff about redemption and him making amends for the treasonable wickedness he'd committed by warning us about the same, but I didn't really follow a lot of it. It's all tied up with him being in purgatory or wherever he is and having to do something or other to get out of the place."

"How extraordinary. He's seeking redemption?"

"Redemption, yes, that's the word he used." Thompson looked at Paget as if the man were a genius. "It was about having to save other people from evil thoughts and deeds so he could be saved himself."

"He didn't specify who he meant?"

"No."

"Nor how this redemption might be worked out?"

"Well, sort of, but he used such big words that I got completely lost. He normally just tells me about the engagements he fought." Thompson seemed suitably ashamed at not having paid attention to the things that would be less appealing to a boy. "He can still cut a caper with his sword. Not that he has a sword, but he makes all the moves."

Paget sighed. Had he been so frivolous as a midshipman, only interested in fighting and battles and missing the important stuff? "So you don't know what he was warning us about?"

"No, sir. Only that it threatened us all."

No point in pursuing that, then. Better to turn away from the paranormal to the all too real matter of murder. "Did you see anyone below decks when you were entertaining your guest?"

"We try to find somewhere we won't be disturbed, sir. That's what the admiral prefers. He says," Thompson lowered his voice conspiratorially, "that he might still have enemies. People who want revenge on him for what he did. Although what they could actually do to him, given his present situation, I don't know."

"Quite." Paget tried not to show his frustration at the way this conversation kept meandering off course. It wasn't the admiral's enemies that bothered him. "You saw nobody?"

"Ah, now I wouldn't say that, sir. I didn't see anyone, but I heard an argument. Two men, voices raised."

Now they were getting somewhere. "Did you recognize the voices?"

"I'm afraid not, sir. I think one of them might have been Ponting, and the other one sounded younger than him, but I couldn't swear to it. And I couldn't rightly hear what was being said. I'm not being a lot of use, am I?" Thompson's lower lip—still as downless as a baby's bottom and a reminder he was barely more than a lad— began to tremble.

"Not at all. You've been very helpful." Paget smiled encouragingly. "Cast your mind back to yesterday. Think about what you heard."

Thompson, eyes shut tight in concentration, said, "They were angry. Like somebody making a threat and somebody else laughing—yes, he was laughing in reply." He looked up, in wide-eyed admiration. "You've helped me remember. That's right—the admiral began to complain about a man not being able to hear himself think with that bloody noise—beg pardon, sir—rattling on. I had to bite my lip to stop myself laughing, as he'd never sworn before. I think I offended the old cove, because he didn't stay long after that."

Paget did some quick mental arithmetic of his own. "So what did you do? Not hare upstairs to see the beast?"

"I would have done had I known, sir." Thompson looked offended. "But like an idiot I sat and had a bit of a think."

"With all that arguing going on?"

"Oh, no, sir. It had stopped by then."

Paget nodded, slowly. "Right. Well, thank you, Mr. Thompson. Back to your sums, now."

The midshipman gave a disappointed salute and went. If he'd told a pack of lies then he was as consummate an actor as any a person might see at Drury Lane. And if he was telling the truth at least one other person had been below decks and none had yet admitted to it.

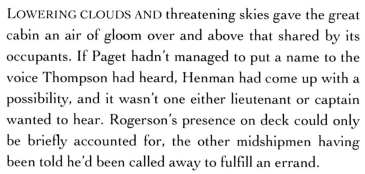

LOWERING CLOUDS AND threatening skies gave the great cabin an air of gloom over and above that shared by its occupants. If Paget hadn't managed to put a name to the voice Thompson had heard, Henman had come up with a possibility, and it wasn't one either lieutenant or captain wanted to hear. Rogerson's presence on deck could only be briefly accounted for, the other midshipmen having been told he'd been called away to fulfill an errand.

"And what did he have to say for himself by way of explanation?" Hopkins asked.

"He said it was a mistake." Henman's narrowed eyes showed what he thought of the story. "He'd thought he was wanted by one of the officers—you, Mr. Paget—but had been in error. He'd watched the monster on his own, not wanting to appear stupid in front of his friends for dreaming you wanted him to perform some task. They tease him for being in awe of you."

"In awe of me? God help him." Paget tried to summon up a smile, but this seemed no laughing matter.

"Maybe you could use that sense of awe to get the truth out of him." Hopkins looked at the notes his officers had made but appeared to find neither enlightenment nor comfort there.

"It might not have been him arguing with Ponting," Henman said, clutching at straws. "You'd have thought Thompson would have definitely recognized his voice."

"You would, but he's at the stage where he can flit between soprano or basso profundo at any two minutes together." Paget felt guilty about acting as devil's advocate, but the truth had to emerge. "I'll question him now."

"No, bear with me a moment. I have another matter to discuss. Thank you, Mr. Henman." Hopkins dismissed the marine.

"Aye, sir." Henman saluted and left them to it.

"Yes?" Paget asked warily. He had a feeling they were about to set off down a path he'd rather leave untrod.

"What do you make of this White Admiral stuff? The message about great evil aboard. Do you believe any of it?" Hopkins drew them as far from the door as could be managed in the confines of the cabin and kept his voice low.

"I believe that Thompson thinks he was told it. I'd have said it was just a lad's imagination, but he seems entirely in earnest." Paget shrugged. "You know, if it lay entirely in his head then surely the whole thing would be less... strange. A ghost who by turns regales him with tales of derring-do and makes dire warnings, when he's not spouting theological matters. It makes no sense." He stared out of the cabin window, unwilling to face his captain's piercing and perceptive gaze.

"What is it you're thinking? Out with it." Hopkins's voice was smooth and tender, but the hard edge to it couldn't be hidden.

"Am I to have no secret thoughts?" Paget grinned, but he felt sick to his stomach. He whispered, "I was wondering if the evil alluded to was... us. Breaking his Majesty's articles of war as often as we get the chance. At risk of bringing scandal to the ship and to the service."

"Do you think we're evil?" Hopkins clasped his hands together as if afraid they might reach out to touch his lover if not kept under control.

Paget looked up, appalled. "Never." He quickly lowered his voice again. "No. Nor do I think we're a threat to the well-being of this ship, or any other we've served aboard. But some people would believe it."

"There's more. I know there is." Hopkins slumped into his seat, head in hands. "You're thinking that my seeing my father's ghost is linked in with this. That he's come back to condemn me."

"No." Paget ached to take Hopkins in his arms and assure him he'd thought no such thing, even though the thought had crossed his mind more than once. To promise him that all would be well, that they'd weathered storms that would make this look like a spring shower,

even though there was the chance they'd founder. "He
was immensely proud of you. Remember that time in
Portsmouth, when your mother dragged you off to look
at items for your sea chest and your father and I shared a
glass of wine? He was fit to burst with tales of what a
fine sailor you were."

"Would he still be proud of me if he knew what we
did that night in my bed?"

Paget took a deep breath. He'd kept a certain coin for
his lover's lowest moment. It seemed the right time to
spend it.

"In amongst all the tales he regaled me with of your
cunning and valor—I think we may have been on our
third glass by then—your father said something quite
extraordinary. That he couldn't describe how much he
valued our friendship. At least that's what I assumed, at
the time, he'd meant, the usual sort of platitude. But
when I remember his exact words, the meaning was
subtly different. 'I cannot express how I value the
particular nature of your friendship to Stephen. It
exceeds all worth.' I can't help thinking he was trying to
say that he knew our relationship went beyond camara-
derie and he literally couldn't express himself in the
circumstances."

Hopkins looked up, the faintest glimmer of hope in
his eyes. "That's just how he would have worded it, if
he'd meant that. This is the truth? You're not just being
kind?"

"Stephen, have we not known each other long and
well enough to see if we're being served a dish of lies?
Even in the cause of kindness? And anyway," Paget

added, smiling, "I hadn't spent enough time with your father to be able to imitate him."

This time Hopkins smiled—a real, almost happy smile. "I was foolish to doubt you."

"You were indeed. If that isn't mutinous talk, implying my captain is a fool."

"We'll call it semi-mutinous and I'll make you pay for it next time we make shore." Hopkins grinned.

"Maybe I should be mutinous more often if that's the punishment."

The captain's grin turned briefly lascivious then was quickly hidden. "Right, back to duty. Back to Ponting. We must do all we can for the man. Not least the final services, which are imminent." He rose from his seat, breathing deeply and girding himself against the ordeal to come. Neither of them liked to commit a man to the deep.

Paget nodded. "And once he's settled, I'll resume my questioning."

"During the service, it might be instructive for you and Douglas to keep watch on the men's faces."

"In case of too pleased a reaction? That sounds sensible."

"Good. I can't have a murderer on my ship, Simon. Nor the uncertainty of my crew looking over their shoulders wondering who might be next. It must be resolved."

"It will be," Paget said with more conviction than he felt.

THERE WAS EVEN less conviction after Ponting had been sent into the arms of his maker. Neither lieutenant nor master had spotted anything untoward among the crew during the service, although the midshipmen had seemed even more unsettled than they normally were at making the final parting with a shipmate. Now the ship had returned to normal, the everyday business of setting sails, keeping watch, and maintaining an orderly vessel.

Paget steered the master towards a quiet corner of the deck and asked, "Might I pick your brains?"

"You may, for all the good they'll do you," Douglas said with good humor.

"Ponting's messmates seemed genuinely sorry to lose him, did they not?"

"Aye, sir. I haven't seen evidence of anything but loss among them."

"You hear these men talk more than I would. What do they say of him?"

"That he was a quiet man. A good sailor and a good friend. As I'd have described him before this. The only thing…"

"Yes?" Paget was keen to hear anything, however small, which might help point the finger of guilt in the right direction, especially if that was away from Rogerson.

"He bore a grudge toward the man who'd had him punished. Not Hardy, but another flogging captain. He said he didn't mind honest punishment, but this had been something else. He felt the man had taken a touch too much pleasure in watching him suffer."

"It happens, alas." Especially if the sailor in question suffered from being too bold or too handsome. Ponting had been both.

"There's more." Douglas lowered his voice. "Last time we touched shore, he'd been in his cups. Started going on about how life might be better under the Frogs. His friends shouted him down, of course, and it all ended amicably enough, but if he voiced those sorts of thoughts with some of the men here…" He shrugged.

"Indeed. Thank you," Paget added, trying not to think of the ruthlessly patriotic streak he'd seen in some of his most valued shipmates. Not least Rogerson.

He left it until the next set of bells before he tackled that young man—enough time for the middie to get over the unease of their shipmate's committal to the deep, but not enough time for him to get his mind entirely clear and his story straight. He found him practicing his knots under his sea daddy's watchful eye. The deck being too busy for private conversation, they went down to the sick bay, which Paget knew was empty and which Cowan had agreed to make available.

"What's this about, sir?" Rogerson asked, an indecipherable look in his eye. Was it fear? Dissembling?

Paget ploughed on. "That evening the monster came. When Ponting died. You followed him below decks and had words with him. We know this. What was the quarrel about?"

Rogerson didn't deny it—maybe, given his awe of Paget, it would seem natural to him that the lieutenant knew so much of what went on. "I wanted to know where he was going and why he was moving—so furtively—against the flow of men. Everyone else wanted to be on deck. I thought it was my duty to find out."

"Go on," Paget said, not wanting to interrupt the flow with either praise or rebuke.

"When I found him in the hold, he said it was none of my business what he was up to. I begged to differ. And then…" Rogerson flushed, full of anger, "he said despicable things. About the captain. Things that couldn't be true."

"What were these things?" The cold spike had reappeared in Paget's spine.

"I couldn't possibly repeat them, sir. Vile slurs."

"I'm sure they're not true. Captain Hopkins is as fine a sailor as ever set foot on a frigate, and I can't believe him capable of anything bad." Paget could say that with confidence, not believing that what they did together was in any way vile. And he'd clearly not been implicated, so maybe he was jumping to the wrong—if obvious—conclusion.

"Exactly, sir. I told him to hold his tongue if he didn't want to end up at the grating, but he just laughed. He said he knew all about being flogged. He'd taken it then and he'd take it now and it wouldn't make a scrap of difference." Rogerson looked supremely uncomfortable.

"What is it? There's more, isn't there?"

The middie swallowed hard. "He'd served under one of those sort of men before. The sort of men he implied the captain is."

Paget clenched his hands, trying not to let his emotions show. The obvious conclusion it was, then. "A wicked implication indeed."

"I know. To compare Mr. Hopkins to a man with no scruples. Ponting said he'd been singled out for harsh treatment because he hadn't..." Rogerson suddenly flushed scarlet and seemed to have lost his ability to speak.

"Hadn't what?" Paget asked, gently, although he could guess the answer.

"Hadn't agreed to be... um... especially friendly... I mean..." The scarlet flush had spread all over the midshipman's face and ears.

"Are you trying to say that Ponting had refused to go to bed with this captain and the man had him punished because of it?" Paget asked.

"Yes, sir," Rogerson said, sighing in relief at being rescued.

"But Ponting didn't imply that Captain Hopkins might do the same thing?"

"Oh, no, sir. He just said he knew by now how to recognize such men, and he was sure the captain was from the same mold."

"This is serious." That was stating the bleeding obvious. "Do you know if he'd told anyone else of his ludicrous suspicions?"

"No, sir. He said he wasn't going to do that until he had all his facts. He said he hadn't got proof yet, but he'd find it one way or another."

Unless somebody stopped him first, of course.

"And what did you say to that? You're a good officer. You'd have stood up for what's right."

"I did, sir. I was furious with him."

"Furious enough to kill?"

SECRETS

"Of course not, sir!" The scarlet flush had become one of indignation, not embarrassment.

"All right, all right," Paget said, raising his hands in surrender in the face of such passionate denial. "But something puzzles me. What was Ponting doing in the hold?"

Rogerson rolled his eyes. "He'd got it into his head that there was a place down there where—by some strange trick of the ship's construction—he'd be able to hear what went on in the captain's cabin. It was part of his wanting proof."

"How extraordinary."

"Madness, I think you might mean, sir, if I can be so bold. Even if you could listen in on the cabin, which I doubt, and if Captain Hopkins was as wicked as Ponting painted him, which I refuse to believe, he's too clever and honest to do anything aboard ship to bring it into disrepute." Rogerson's lower lip began to waver. "He loves Hecuba, sir."

"Of course he does. As do we all."

So Rogerson had clearly thought this through, and he'd been spot on with his conclusion. Paget could—had it been in any way appropriate—have reassured him that Hopkins would never make a mess on his own doorstep. Even kisses were kept for behind thick wooden doors, ashore. Ponting must have been clutching at straws, desperate to find any way to have his theory vindicated.

"Rogerson, you've always struck me as a man of your word." Even though those words might be spoken in a voice that veered between a man's and a boy's. "Do you swear that Ponting was still alive when you left him?

29

Alive and well and having suffered no injuries?" Paget added, closing the loophole.

"I swear it, sir. I'll lay my hand on the Bible and say it if you want."

"No need for that. There's no place where God's not already our witness."

"Then I'll state it again, sir. We argued, but I didn't lay a hand on him."

And Paget felt largely convinced that he hadn't laid a belaying pin on the man, either.

PAGET STOPPED BY the taffrail, trying to get his thoughts clear. Thompson's admiral had warned of evil—was that about his relationship with the captain, or Ponting's plans to expose Hopkins's nature, or simply the murderous urge that lay in someone or other's heart? He almost wished the admiral would manifest himself now, on the deck, so he could cross examine him.

Better to stick with the people he could interrogate. Rogerson had been the man arguing, unless there'd been another who came after. But why multiply entities unnecessarily? Thompson had only mentioned one argument. Except there must have been somebody else in the offing, the man who'd whacked Ponting, unless he'd done the thing to himself. Was that even possible? The wound had been on the side of the temple, after all.

Paget just managed to stop himself recreating the action required. No point in risking the crew thinking their first lieutenant had gone mad in the face of all the strange occurrences which had beset them.

And why would Ponting kill himself anyway? The man had a mission to fulfill, even if that mission was evil in thought and deed.

Evil thoughts and deeds.

Somebody else had used those words, somebody who'd been down below at the time Ponting was killed. Somebody who'd been guilty of treasonable wickedness himself. Had Paget been chasing the wrong vessel all this time? Was it Ponting's treacherous talk about France which had made him a victim?

And was Paget being a fool for considering asking Thompson if the White Admiral could open doors and pick up objects as well as walk through the ship's walls?

WHEN PAGET LOCATED THOMPSON, the lad looked as though he'd lost a sovereign and found a groat.

"Are you feeling quite well?" Paget said, sitting beside him on the bench.

"Yes, sir. It's just… he's gone, sir."

"Who's gone?" Paget wasn't sure his poor brain could cope with any further complications, alarms, or incidents.

"The White Admiral. He came this morning to say goodbye. He said he'd done his duty to King and country as he should have done it for his Queen, so his work was done."

What work? And had it involved that belaying pin? "He didn't tell you what that work was?"

"No, sir. He just said I'd been a good lad for listening to him and that I'd hoist my admiral's flag rather than being hoisted at the yardarm so long as I knew where my loyalties lay."

"Your loyalties lie with your ship, first and foremost, so that's excellent advice." Paget chose his words carefully. "I've never met a ghost, so you have the advantage of me. Would you say that he was capable of, let us say, handling earthly objects? Or was he all spirit and no substance?"

"Ah, that I can tell you. I once asked him to show me some of his swordplay with a real weapon, because I wanted to learn how to have as deft a hand as his, but he said that he normally couldn't use something from our dominion. 'Only in extreme circumstances and for the greater good.' That's what he said."

If getting rid of Ponting had been an extreme circumstance, and for the greater good, then maybe his death had hastened the admiral's redemption.

"YOU'RE HONESTLY TELLING ME you believe Ponting was killed by this ghost of an admiral." Hopkins clearly didn't believe a word of it.

"It seems the only solution. Henman and I just conferred, and every other man jack is accounted for except Rogerson and Thompson. And Cowan reckons there'd have likely been blood on one or the other of them if they'd done the deed." Paget had checked and doubled checked, wanting as watertight a case as he could present.

"And do either of them accept your identification of the murderer?"

"They haven't had the chance. It's only right you should know first."

"Hm." Hopkins rose from his chair, turning to look out of the stern window. "What do you propose we tell the crew?"

"What we've told them so far. That we're satisfied Ponting's death was a terrible accident. Or perhaps self inflicted. Guilt over his treasonable thoughts."

"Stick with the accident. It's more convincing."

"It'll have to be convincing or they'll all mutiny!" Paget raised his hand to stem his captain's protest. "If we've missed something obvious and let a murderer go free then the crew can't know that."

"I know," Hopkins said after an awkward pause. "And if he strikes again then we'll be left in no doubt of our error."

"I've thought of that, Stephen. Believe me."

THREE WEEKS HAD PASSED. Three weeks without monsters or ghosts or anything worse than unwashed midshipmen affecting the ship. Three weeks in which no further incidents happened, apart from the taking of a pair of French corvettes, which raised the crew's spirits and turned everyone's minds from Ponting's demise to prize money.

It had taken most of those three weeks for Paget to work out the best way of asking the question he needed to, yet dreaded. A good dinner shared in the great cabin, excellent coffee and dessert to follow, created the sort of atmosphere that it was a shame to spoil — and which would be conducive to candor.

"Will I need to look for a priest when we hit Plymouth?" Paget asked, blithely, while he peeled an orange, one of the literal fruits of their recent successes.

"Only to absolve you of your manifold sins and wickedness," Hopkins replied, cradling his coffee and rocking with the easy movement of the ship. "I spoke to Thompson and his friend's still not been back. Clearly he has been redeemed, so perhaps your outlandish theory is vindicated. I think Rogerson misses him."

"I bet he does. When I was a boy I'd have relished that sort of thing. No other ghosts who'd need gently persuading to move on?"

"No. I've not seen him since that last time, when he was here in the cabin." No need to say who he was. "Funnily enough, I miss him, too. I thought I'd be glad of his being gone, but I miss seeing his face again. And his smile."

"A smiling ghost? You never told me that."

"As you said, am I to have no secrets?" Hopkins savored his port.

"Only those we must keep from the rest of the world." Paget watched him drink, fondly. He'd been incubating a new theory these last few weeks. If ghosts could use earthly weapons in extremis, then that rule would surely apply not just to the White Admiral but to other spirits, as well.

If Ponting was about to expose Hopkins to disgrace, then another spirit had a motive to get rid of the man before he could speak out. A spirit with a deep, abiding affection for Hopkins, one who valued his friendship with Paget rather than decried it. Maybe that other ghost had even worked in concert with the admiral, two spirits steering a joint course to redemption.

He looked out the window to the sea—the wonderfully calm sea, which didn't reflect his inner turmoil. Should he tell Stephen what he suspected or keep it buried within his heart? He'd long been prepared to sacrifice everything for his captain, for his lover. His right arm, his life if need be, and perhaps, now, his peace of mind.

Paget raised his glass. "To secrets. Long may we have them."

Hopkins raised his port, too. "To secrets."

CONSTANCE AND CONSPIRACY

by
Helen Angove

THE PRESENCE AND ASSISTANCE of a rational and competent gentleman is indispensible in a crisis—the wisdom of the world has it so, and the wisdom of the world is never wrong.

Miss Ellen Balinburgh had to admit that the presence of Sir Marcus Blaine was indescribably comforting. In one terrifying bolt of ill fortune she had been rendered friendless and soon to be homeless. Sir Marcus had been sent for, had arrived post-haste, and was even now epitomizing reason and competence in the library.

"I realize that this must be most distressing for you, Miss Balinburgh," he was saying, his voice gentle, "but I must ask you to describe to me, to the best of your ability, the events of last night."

Ellen took a deep breath.

"I was attending Miss Blaine as she made her preparations to retire," she said. Her voice shook. "She had but moments before taken to her bed, and…"

Sir Marcus raised his hand to stop her. "A moment," he said. "This was in the master bed chamber?"

"Yes, Sir Marcus. In the mahogany bed with the brass knobs on the posts."

Sir Marcus nodded. "I know the one."

Ellen continued. "I blew out the candle. The room was completely dark and quiet. There was nothing— nothing to warn us! The great flash of light seemed to come out of nowhere, there was a mighty noise, and I—I am not sure what happened, but I was swept from my feet and I found myself slammed against the wall, my breath dashed from my body!" She paused, the memory of the events, still so fresh in her mind, rendering her unable to continue speaking.

"I must ask you to be brave, Miss Balinburgh," said Sir Marcus. "What happened next?"

"For a moment I was too bewildered to move. I could see nothing: the brightness of the light had blinded me. I then called out to Constance—to Miss Blaine—but she gave no reply."

Again, Ellen was forced to pause. The horror of the night was still upon her: the dreadful fear that had gripped her heart when Constance had not replied! She had scrambled to her feet and made her way to the bed, had grasped the arm of what lay there, had shaken it, but had elicited no response. It was not, however, until her trembling hands had found the candle and had succeeded in lighting it from the decaying embers of the fire that she was forced to confront the dreadful truth: Constance lying dead, the covers blown off her body, her eyes wide with shock but sightless, and no sign of damage but a red mark on her right temple! The memory of it was too much. Ellen placed her face in her hands, and began to weep.

Sir Marcus was at once solicitous. "I have asked too much of you, Miss Balinburgh," he said. "I know that the friendship between you and my cousin was far stronger than that usually found between companion and employer. You need not continue, I have seen the body."

"What could have caused such a thing to happen?"

Sir Marcus sat up a little straighter, his expression determined. "I do not know, but I intend to find out. It is my duty, both as a cousin and as a Justice of the Peace. I shall investigate this matter, you may be sure of that."

"Could it have been some kind of—of lightning? It was a stormy night. But the window was closed."

"And the house is protected by a Franklin rod," replied Sir Marcus.

"I seem to remember Miss Blaine saying something about that to me, once," said Ellen, "although I paid little attention at the time. I never shared her interest in natural philosophy."

"Even with all this?" Sir Marcus indicated the apparatus that stood on the table behind him, one of many such assemblages of equipment in the room.

Ordinarily Ellen might have laughed. At the moment she could manage, at best, a sad smile. "Even with all of this," she said, gazing at the utensil on the table, a wooden box containing a collection of uniform jars, the top of each one connected to the next by means of copper rods. "I do not even know to what use this device was put. But I believe we must be careful when we move it. Miss Blaine warned me several times not to touch it."

"Then care shall indeed be taken," said Sir Marcus, "for I understand little of natural philosophy or scientific method myself. Indeed, my poor late cousin's fascination with the study was always a matter of some mystery to me. A strange occupation for a woman."

"Miss Blaine was of independent means and had no one to please but herself."

"That is true enough. But to return to the subject in hand, I had understood that should a house protected by a Franklin rod be hit by lightning, the electrical fluid will

CONSTANCE AND CONSPIRACY

pass harmlessly down the rod to the ground, leaving no
damage be—"

But whatever it was that Sir Marcus was saying was
suddenly interrupted with a thunderous knocking sound.
Ellen, still overwrought from the events of the previous
night, could not help but utter a scream, and even Sir
Marcus started and looked about him.

"What in the devil was that?" he cried, and, as if in
reply, the knocking came again.

"It seems to be coming from the drawing room!"
cried Ellen.

Leaping up from his seat, Sir Marcus took up his
cane, and hurried from the room. Ellen followed at a
distance, and was in time to see him fling open the doors
of the drawing room—only to find it empty. He swung
around to face Ellen, and seemed about to speak, when
again came the deafening knocking—this time seemingly
from the hallway. Again, Sir Marcus followed the
sound—again the room was empty!

Sir Marcus turned about the spot, but the hallway
was devoid of all features other than a rosewood jardinière supporting a vase of chrysanthemums. Again he
opened his mouth to speak—his eyes twitched, he looked
to be in some discomfort—his hand went to the tail
pocket of his coat—and then his face was convulsed by
the agitation of a powerful sneeze.

"I do beg your pardon, Miss Balinburgh," he said,
once he was able to speak again. "A touch of summer
catarrh, nothing more."

"Miss Blaine was subject to the same complaint," said
Ellen. "She had, through the careful recording of her

symptoms and the associated circumstances, come to believe that the affliction was exacerbated by the presence of flowering plants. Perhaps you would do well to move away from the chrysanthemums."

"An interesting theory," replied Sir Marcus. "I shall try it."

Suiting action to the word, Sir Marcus approached the grand staircase, Ellen not far behind. But even then they encountered no sign as to the author of the strange knocking until they were past the corner of the stairs, whereupon they came across the footman coming down towards them, a silver tray in his hand.

"Thomas! Did you see anyone below just now? Has anyone come this way?" cried Sir Marcus.

"No, indeed, sir, I did not," replied Thomas, looking positively alarmed at the intensity of Sir Marcus's demeanor.

No more could any of the other servants, upon being questioned, give any explanation to the knocking sounds, although many of the servants had heard them. Sir Marcus was obliged to confess himself quite bewildered. "I shall investigate, however," he said. "You may be sure of that!"

IT WAS AGREED that Sir Marcus should remain at Blaine House until after the funeral, and Ellen, distressed by so many unexplained events, was not sorry that it should be so. Constance, she remembered, had always liked and trusted her cousin, and his presence was an undoubted comfort.

"In time, my dear," said Sir Marcus, "we must address the question of your future. I will not be responsible for turning a friendless woman out into the world. Do you have anywhere to go?"

Ellen sighed. "There is my brother's house," she said, "although I fear his wife will not welcome me. I suppose I shall have to look about for a new situation."

"I will see to it that you have the best of references," replied Sir Marcus. "And I will make enquiries as well. I am sure that a suitable situation will present itself. Moreover, once my cousin's estate is wound up, I feel sure that there will be some small amount from which an annuity might be found. You will not be forgotten."

"Thank you, Sir Marcus. I am grateful that you should think of me. But Miss Blaine always said you had a good heart. She said that you were the only one of her family who stood up for her when she refused to marry Mr. Thorne."

"Of course I must think of you. Constance would have desired nothing less."

But at the mention of her friend's name, Ellen once again found that the tears began to flow.

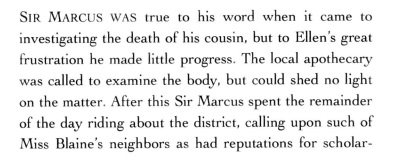

SIR MARCUS WAS true to his word when it came to investigating the death of his cousin, but to Ellen's great frustration he made little progress. The local apothecary was called to examine the body, but could shed no light on the matter. After this Sir Marcus spent the remainder of the day riding about the district, calling upon such of Miss Blaine's neighbors as had reputations for scholarship—but none were able to shed any light upon the mysterious circumstances of the recent accident. In the mean time a myriad of practical things had to be done: the body must be laid out, the undertaker instructed with regard to the coffin, the vicar consulted about the funeral, letters written and the neighborhood advised; and naturally these tasks fell to Ellen.

It was therefore not until dinner that Ellen next saw Sir Marcus. He was clearly tired from riding, and Ellen herself had little appetite for either food or conversation. Sir Marcus exerted himself, however, to ask solicitously after her day, and Ellen found she was able to respond in kind. The meal therefore, although taken mostly in silence, was not an ordeal.

Not an ordeal, that was, until suddenly they were interrupted by another great noise! A noise, moreover, that was not from the next room, this time, but from their own: for a large picture that hung over the fireplace — although no one had touched it or even stood near — suddenly fell from its hook and crashed to the floor!

Ellen came close to fainting; even Sir Marcus turned pale. "By the devil!" he cried. "What is this?" But the question, although remarkably pertinent to the circumstances, remained unanswered.

EXHAUSTED AND PRACTICALLY DISTRAUGHT, Ellen retired early that night. Gripping the candlestick with white-knuckled hands, she made her way to the attic room that had been assigned to her upon her first arrival in Miss Blaine's employ. The room was cold and unwelcoming, but she nevertheless made her toilette, blew out the candle, and slipped under the covers.

But her repose was short lived. Suddenly, out of the darkness, once again came the thunderous knocking! It seemingly came first from one corner of the room, then from another. From time to time it paused, and Ellen, cowering in the dark, hoped it had ended, but then it would begin again in a new place.

Eventually she could stand it no more. Taking hold of all the courage she could muster, Ellen threw back the covers, fled from the room, and ran down the dark staircase to Constance's old bedchamber. It might have been the room in which her employer had died, but it was also the room which had seen the happiest memories of the friend she had lost.

The servants had not yet stripped the bed. Soon, the heavy damask curtains would be taken down, and the beautiful velvet Persian bedspread with the silver embroidery would be packed away with cedar and lavender. For now, however, the bed remained untouched, other than having been tidied after Constance's body had been moved, and Ellen stretched herself across it and cried herself to sleep.

AFTER HAVING WOKEN from a cold and restless night, Ellen felt exhausted and again had little appetite, but she felt it was nonetheless incumbent upon her to attend Sir Marcus at breakfast. The situation was awkward. She was not the mistress of the house, but neither was he yet the master, and it was not clear who was guest and who host, but the rules of good conduct, she was sure, required some kind of intercourse between them at the beginning of the day. Accordingly she made her way to the breakfast parlor.

The door to the parlor was closed as Ellen approached, but the muted sound of voices within suggested that Sir Marcus was already at his meal. She approached the door, touched the doorknob—and then sprang back with a great cry of distress and alarm! For as she had touched the cold metal, a sensation—a sudden, stinging jolt of extraordinary intensity—had seized her whole body, momentarily robbing her limbs of their strength!

Within moments, Sir Marcus and Thomas had burst from the room and come to her aid, guiding her to a chair and fetching the salts. For some minutes she was too distressed to speak. But even when she was able to describe her experience, Sir Marcus was unable to shed any light upon the phenomenon she had just experienced.

"What can this be?" she cried. "These strange occurrences, the knocking, the falling of the picture? What can they mean?"

He looked grave. "I can no longer pretend that I am doing any good here," he said. "I am baffled, wholly baffled. Despite all my questions, of the servants, the neighbors, I have discovered nothing."

Ellen clutched at his arm. "You will not leave?"

He turned his eyes towards hers. "Not if you do not wish me to."

"I cannot help but feel that—that there is some malevolent presence here. Something—something that wishes me gone."

"You suspect—a supernatural explanation?"

Ellen had been prevented from voicing her suspicions earlier by the fear of inciting Sir Marcus's contempt. But now, at last, desperation forced the words from her.

Sir Marcus did not laugh. Instead he regarded her with all seriousness. "As a rational man," he said, "I find it hard to countenance such ideas. And yet—and yet I can think of no other explanation."

"I shall write to my brother," said Ellen, with a heavy heart, "and make my preparations to leave."

"Perhaps it would be as well," he replied. "But will you allow me to enquire after you, once you are established in your brother's household? It would be of great benefit to my peace of mind to know you are well established."

Ellen heard the words with amazement. To receive such an attention from such a one as Sir Marcus—could it mean what she thought it meant? And yet it was perhaps not so strange: although she was past the first bloom of youth, Ellen knew herself to still be considered remarkably handsome, and Sir Marcus was of an age when he might be supposed to have long since been ready to take a wife. Matches of greater inequality had taken place.

If her suspicions were justified, how, then, did she feel about it? She truly was not certain—it was so sudden—but common courtesy required some reply. "Thank you," she said. "That would be most kind."

FOR ALL THE COMFORT of Sir Marcus's continued presence, the distressing nature of the day continued without relief. Any room in which she established herself was soon afterward disturbed by the violent knocking, and there were other strange occurrences too: in the breakfast parlor the fire, suddenly and without warning, quenched itself; in another room the window sash fell with a loud crash that made her heart race. She began to seriously consider the possibility that she might have to quit the house earlier than she had hoped, and impose herself upon her brother without even the little warning a letter would have afforded.

The immediate chores of death having been completed, Ellen began the melancholy duty of making the rounds of the house, collecting together the many items of her possession that had insinuated themselves into its rooms. It was hard for her to countenance the fact that this place she had learned to call home would not be so for very much longer.

As she made the tour of the rooms, her task was made the more poignant by her happening across many of the servants, each of them engaged in their proper activities according to the day and hour. Faithful retainers all, these people had long been part of her life. It was a bittersweet thing to encounter Thomas hurrying through the passage, his arms filled with a device that she recognized as coming from Constance's collection of scientific apparatus in the library: the wooden box filled with the jars that Sir Marcus had remarked upon the previous day.

"Why, Thomas," she exclaimed, "whatever are you doing with that?"

He looked embarrassed. "Sir Marcus told me to put it in the stable loft, Miss Balinburgh." His words caused her a pang, but Ellen could not be surprised. Sir Marcus would come into possession of the house soon enough, and he would have no use for Constance's scientific instruments.

Ellen found herself in the library, although the books therein belonged all to the house, her own property in the room being limited to a penwiper and a profile of Constance, her own work, that had been hung above the mantelpiece. Once in the room, however, she found herself lingering. This room had been such a favorite of Constance's, a place where she had spent many hours in experimentation, and in perusal of the works of scientific discovery she had loved so well. Almost without awareness of her actions, Ellen found herself sitting at the desk, gazing at the shelves of books around her.

The day was fine, and the windows had been opened to air the room. The curtains blew gently in the breeze causing an irregular scrap of sunlight to flicker on the shelves, and Ellen found her eye drawn towards it.

Was it her imagination, or did the beam of light fall particularly upon the spine of one specific book? It must be her fancy, and yet she could not entirely shake the notion.

There was nothing especially remarkable about the book: it was bound in red leather, the title tooled in gold upon the spine, and it was in neither better condition nor more foxed than its fellows. And yet Ellen could not quite resist the urge to fetch it from the shelf.

Conversations on Electricity read the title. Ellen opened it up and, carelessly enough at first, began to leaf through the pages.

She might have returned the book to its place had not her attention been arrested by a reproduction of an engraving of two men, apparently being blown backwards off their feet by what appeared to be a bolt of light. This image, and the similarity it bore to Ellen's own recent experience, could hardly fail to arrest her, and she feverishly turned her attention to the accompanying text.

The book took the form of conversations between a governess and her pupils, the latter asking questions about the import of the engraving. The gentlemen in the picture, the governess explained, were one Georg Wilhelm Richmann and an engraver who had been retained to record the results of Professor Richmann's scientific research. The professor had heard thunder and had rushed back to his lodgings in order to conduct experiments. He had been attempting to use a fifty-foot-long vertical insulated rod to draw down the electrical fluid of the lightning. While the experiment was in progress, however, a great incandescent bolt of electrical charge had darted down the rod and leapt through the air to his head, killing him outright. Moreover—and it was upon reading this that Ellen gasped aloud—the only sign of damage to his body had been a red spot on his forehead, and some marks of singeing on his clothes!

Could this be the explanation she had been searching for? Casting down her book she leapt to her feet and

positively ran through the house to Constance's bedchamber. Reaching the bed she pulled back the curtains
and fell to her knees to examine the bedspread. Although
the dark fabric and the embroidery obscured it, the
evidence was there for anyone to see: dark scorch marks
traversing the length of the fabric!

Sir Marcus was still abroad making calls, she knew.
He might not be home for some hours yet, so she could
neither tell him of her discovery nor discuss with him the
mysteries that yet remained. She could not rest, however,
with so many questions unanswered.

Among these was the mystery of how, if Sir Marcus
was right about the protective value of a Franklin rod,
the accident had come to pass. Determined to satisfy
herself on this point at least, Ellen made her way back to
the library to continue her perusal of the book.

The book, it transpired, had been written as a primer
on the subject of electricity, modeled on the famous
introductory science texts of Mrs. Marcet. As a result,
even with no prior knowledge of natural philosophy,
Ellen found she could understand it with little effort.

She read of Professors Galvani and Volta and their
debates on the subject of animal electricity. She read of
Dr. Benjamin Franklin and his experiments with lightning—a key, borne aloft on a kite in a thunderstorm!—
and then, finally, came across a description of his invention, the Franklin rod.

The principle was not difficult to grasp. A metal rod
attached to a tall building would act in such a way as to,
in a storm, draw the electrical fire from the clouds, which

would in this way be conducted harmlessly to the earth, causing damage to neither person nor property.

What, in that case, could have transpired that dreadful night in Constance's bedchamber? What had gone wrong?

Ellen resolved to inspect the rod herself. Fetching her shawl, she made her way onto the terrace, from which vantage point she knew she could see it. And it was not hard to see: a thick copper bar, stained green with verdigris, bolted on to the brickwork of the chimney. From there it traversed the slope of the roof down past a dormer window, whereupon it was hidden from view, by a second dormer window, of the story below.

Ellen shifted her position, convinced she had seen all she needed to see. As, however, her eye fell upon the rod from a different angle—and she could see a portion of it that could not be seen from any other vantage point—she realized that it was not continuous. The rod was visible again lower down the wall, but where its path was hidden from most angles by the dormer there was an extensive gap!

Ellen frowned. If she had understood her book correctly, in order to work the rod must extend continuously to the ground. Moreover, it then occurred to her that the window of the dormer at which the rod disappeared was the very window of Constance's bedchamber!

She hastened back into the house, and up the stairs. Opening the door of the bedchamber she could see at once that the room had been altered: the bed had been stripped, and the curtains taken down. The top of the bed, once largely hidden by a profusion of draperies, was bare—and attached to the brass ball on the top of one of the bedposts at the head of the bed was a thick copper wire, a wire that extended the short way to the wall, and then disappeared into the plaster!

Now, thanks to her recent reading, she understood. The Franklin rod must have attracted a bolt of lightning, which had then traveled down the rod and through the wire to the bed knob. There, however, it was stayed, for the posts of the bed were wooden, and electricity, she now knew, does not traverse dry wood. It would take the path of the least resistance to the ground, and the path of the least resistance would have been through the air to Constance's head, and then—of course!—through the metallic embroidery on the bedspread, thence to travel by means unknown through the rest of the house and to the earth.

Even in the midst of the excitement of having deduced the truth, however, Ellen was struck by a terrible thought. For the deliberate fragmentation of the Franklin rod, the wire passed through the wall—all this spoke of premeditation, which in turn, spoke of—murder!

Who could have done such a thing? What kind of cold-blooded individual could set such a trap, and then be content to wait, not knowing when, or even if, it might be sprung? The evidence surely pointed to someone in the house, for who else could have had opportunity to interfere with the Franklin rod?

A noise below alerted her to the return of Sir Marcus, and she hastened down the stairs to tell him of her discoveries. At first her excitement could hardly allow her to form coherent words, and Sir Marcus was obliged to lead her into the parlor and pour her a glass of wine. When at last, however, she succeeded in making herself understood, he was most gratifyingly impressed. "It must be as you have said," he told her. "I can see no fault in your reasoning. And yet who could have done such a thing?"

"I do not know. One of the servants? But to the best of my knowledge, Miss Blaine had not an enemy in the world."

"No more she had. But Miss Balinburgh —"

"Sir Marcus?"

"Miss Balinburgh. I have never met a woman like you. You have not, perhaps, been unaware of my grow-ing admiration for you, even over the short time we have been acquainted. I have the greatest respect for you, and the way in which you have borne yourself over this whole affair. These deductions of yours have been but the final touch of perfection. This is perhaps neither the time nor the place, but my feelings will brook no further delay. In short, Miss Balinburgh, would you do me the very great honor of consenting to become my wife?"

Ellen was, very literally, struck dumb. Her surprise was so great that she could utter not so much as a sound. Aware she might have been of some admiration on the part of Sir Marcus, but in no way had she expected it to lead him to such a pitch, so soon!

It had been some years since Ellen had given any thought to the subject of marriage. She was entirely without portion, and had never had anything but her looks to recommend her; she had never had high hopes of finding herself established. Moreover, the recent years she had spent in the home of her friend had been so happy as to render negligible any appeal the marital state had ever held for her, and she had ceased entirely to seek it.

Now, however, all was different. She had lost her employment, was about to lose her home. Very soon she would be penniless and virtually friendless. And here she was being offered everything—security, position in society, wealth—by a gentleman who had proved himself unfailingly considerate.

She forced herself to speak. "Sir Marcus," she began, her voice sounding strange in her ears, "I am greatly honored. But this is so sudden—my friend so recently dead—I do not wish to seem ungrateful—"

Sir Marcus smiled. "Forgive me. I have spoken too soon. Of course you are not ready yet to give me your reply. I can wait, Miss Balinburgh."

"Thank you, Sir Marcus."

ELLEN SPENT THE NIGHT in some considerable confusion of mind. She did not know what to do, what reply to give. She wished she could talk to Constance, her confidante for so long, and receive her counsel. As soon as it was light, desperate for distraction, she returned to her perusal of the science textbook from the library.

She read of Ewald Georg von Kliest, the Bishop of Pomerania, and his experiments with Leyden jars: how he had lined a glass jar with silver foil and charged the device using a friction machine. He had once, by accident, touched the jar after it had been charged: the result had been a jolt of extraordinary sensation, a sudden universal blow throughout his whole body, from head to foot. She read of how this effect might be compounded by use of a battery of jars connected together, and she studied the illustration provided of one such "battery".

The illustration was familiar. She looked at it again. Did it not look remarkably like the piece of apparatus she had seen Thomas carrying out to the stable loft only the previous day? And—now she thought of it—did not her experience upon touching the doorknob of the breakfast parlor seem remarkably like that of the bishop upon touching the Leyden jar? Could Constance's jars have somehow been charged and attached to the knob on the other side of the door?

The evidence pointed to Thomas. But why should Thomas have done such a thing? She had always thought him such a loyal servant! Ellen thought back over the strange events of the last couple of days. The falling of the picture, the slamming down of the window sash, the quenching of the fire, the strange knocking—was not every one of those phenomena entirely susceptible to forgery? In fact, had not Thomas been found nearby during the first occurrence of the knocking?

She remembered that he had been found on the stairs with a silver tray on that occasion: somewhere he had no business to be at that time of the morning, and why would he have had need of a tray when there was nothing to be carried? If, on the other hand, he had run there quickly after the perpetration of the uncanny noises, with the tray as an excuse for his presence…

The house was still quiet; it was too early for even the servants to be awake. Dressing quickly and stealing through the silent house, Ellen made her way to the breakfast parlor. The fire had not yet been made up: the ashes of the day before remained in the grate. Bending down, Ellen peered up the chimney.

There was some kind of apparatus up there! A shallow pan, bearing traces of a cargo of ash, had been fixed to the inside of the flue by means of an iron bar wedged across the width of the chimney. One side of the pan had been attached to the bar with rough hinges of wire, and the other hung free, a length of dark twine leading from it out into the room. It was not hard to see how the pan, filled with old ashes, might have been wedged into place and then dislodged by an unseen agent by means of the dark string, discharging its load over the fire and smothering it.

Here was proof indeed. Ellen realized that her intuition had not been wrong. There was a malignant presence in the house that desired her removal, but it was not supernatural in origin. But why should Thomas, of all people, wish to do such a thing?

She sat herself upon the settle to think. She could not bring to mind any reason for there to be bad blood between Thomas and herself—she could not recall ever having done him a disservice, and he had never voiced dissatisfaction with his position. Moreover, assuming all the strange recent events to be connected, how could he have ever been in a position to meddle with the Franklin rod? It seemed that whatever answers she found in this mystery merely raised more questions.

She raised her eyes to the window. A late butterfly—a tortoiseshell—was fluttering around the window. As she watched it, it appeared to give up its attempts to escape through the closed sash and struck out instead across the room. She followed it with her eyes.

It alighted upon Constance's old desk. Moved to pity, Ellen opened the window, and then approached the insect with the hope of shooing it back out into the open air.

But the creature showed a stubborn determination to remain where it was. Every time she beat at the air around it, it would flutter up into the air, but then come down again onto the same spot, poised directly above a particular drawer.

Ellen wondered if there was something in the drawer that could be attracting it. Some lump sugar, perhaps, carelessly dropped when being added to a cup of tea. She pulled the drawer open, but it was filled only with old letters and papers. Wondering if whatever was attracting the butterfly was somewhere below, she lifted the mass out of the drawer and onto the desk.

There was nothing in the drawer, but now the insect was fluttering above the pile of papers on the desk. As Ellen watched, it alighted once again. Once again she tried to shoo it towards the window, but once again it showed a stubborn determination to keep returning to the same spot.

The paper on which the butterfly had landed was an old letter. She pulled it from the pile and looked at it more closely—perhaps some sweet tea had at some point been spilled upon the paper. But there were no stains to suggest such a thing had happened.

Catching sight of the heading, she realized that it was a letter from Sir Marcus to Constance. Without really meaning to, she found herself reading the first few lines.

My dear Constance, she read. *I am most happy to be in receipt of your thanks for my help and my gifts, but I must protest that the gratitude you express is far in excess of my deserts. The bed and the bedspread belonged to our grandmother, and I feel sure that she would have wished them to belong to a woman who would appreciate them for the beautiful things they are, rather than to an old bachelor who cares only that his bed is comfortable and free of draughts! As for the other thing, I have long had dealings with the company of Huddy and Sons, and have always found them to be honest and reliable, and I know them to have some experience in the art of installing Franklin rods. I am very glad to hear that my recommendation of them bore fruit.*

Ellen found she could hardly breathe. Sir Marcus was linked, linked most certainly to the incongruities surrounding Constance's death! Could he be the author of all the strange events of the last few days? She had thought him an honorable gentleman; could he truly be capable of planning a cold-blooded murder, and of trying to frighten her from the house while at the same time making love to her?

The butterfly had settled itself down once more upon the pile of papers upon the desk, now upon a different paper. Ellen could hardly believe herself capable of such credulity, but the draw of the insect's uncanny prescience was beyond her power to resist. Once again, she picked up the paper on which the creature had settled.

It was an envelope, sealed with wax. She turned it over. The writing on the front, in Constance's familiar hand, read "The Last Will and Testament of Constance Blaine."

A will? Constance had never mentioned a will, and Sir Marcus, as her next of kin, had not betrayed any knowledge of such a thing.

Ellen could not have restrained herself. She broke the seal, opened the document, and read.

In the name of God Amen.

I, Constance Blaine of the parish of Saint Luke in the County of Middlesex, spinster, being of sound and perfect mind and memory (praise be God for the same) do make and ordain this my last Will and Testament in manner and form following: That is to say, first and principally I commend my soul into the hands of Almighty God my creator, hoping through the merits of Jesus Christ to obtain pardon and remission of all my sins and to inherit everlasting life, and my body I commit to the earth to be devoutly buried at the discretion of my executor hereafter named. As to the worldly goods which God has given me, I give and dispose thereof as followeth. I give and bequeath to my beloved friend Ellen Balinburgh all my money in the stocks in the Bank of England. Likewise I give to my foresaid beloved friend my house, all the effects thereof. I make my cousin, Sir Marcus Blaine, my full and whole executor.

Constance Blaine

*Signed, sealed, published, and delivered by the said Con-
stance Blaine the testatrix, as and for her last Will and
Testament in the presence of us who at her bequest in her
presence and in the presence of each other have subscribed
our names as witnesses:*

Marcus Blaine,

Thomas Smith.

There could be no doubt of the legality of the document. It was signed by Constance's own hand, and
witnessed by Sir Marcus and Thomas the footman!

Ellen felt an icy chill through her whole body. How
could there be any doubt? She had been the victim of a
conspiracy. Sir Marcus was not the disinterested friend
she had taken him for; clearly, neither was he as ignorant
of natural philosophy as he had claimed. Presumably he
was also not as wealthy as he was reputed to be, for she
could only deduce he had long coveted his cousin's
property!

Moreover, his recent proposal took upon it a new and
sinister meaning: at first he had tried to frighten her
away whilst being careful to gain her sympathy, but then,
as she started to divine some of the truth, he had tried to
bring her more firmly under his power. Perhaps he had
even thought so far ahead as to consider the fact that the
law does not allow a wife to testify against her husband?
She knew him—now—to be capable of thinking and
planning far ahead. It was a chilling thought. What was
she to do?

She felt paralyzed by fear and the aftershock of betrayal. She must quit the house, that was certain, for
what might Sir Marcus do to her once he realized she

understood his guilt? But how? And where should she go?

She might have sat there for hours, only she was interrupted by the sound of the door being opened. It was Thomas, bearing the linen and china to lay the breakfast table. He started with surprise when he saw her, but when he saw the will lying open in her lap, his face went wholly white. He staggered backwards, and sank down into a chair.

While the shock seemed to enervate Thomas, to Ellen it acted as a stimulant. She leapt to her feet. To her great surprise, her voice was steady as she held out the will and asked: "What is the meaning of this, Thomas?"

Thomas pressed his hand to his eyes. "Sir Marcus said I'd lose my job if I didn't do what he said! He said he'd throw me out without so much as a reference!"

"Oh, Thomas. What would Miss Blaine have said?"

At the mention of his former mistress, any remaining assurance of Thomas's fled. He groaned. "I'm sorry, Miss, I'm so sorry! I didn't ought to have done it, but there's mother to think on. What'd she do without my wages?"

Ellen softened a little. She had forgotten that Thomas had a blind mother, dependent on him for her living. "Perhaps we can yet make this right," she said. "Thomas, go down to the stables and have the bay mare saddled for me."

"The bay mare?" Thomas's eyes were wide.

"Yes," snapped Ellen. "Because I only ever rode the gray pony, you think I am not a horsewoman?" In truth, she was not as confident as she sounded, but she felt that

she might have need of a fast horse before the hour was
out.

IF ELLEN WAS to quit the house, she would need riding
clothes and her purse. Accordingly, treading as quietly as
she could, she made her way to her chamber to change.

She must also safeguard the letter and the will. Having found them, Ellen did not wish them to leave her
possession again. In desperation, as she changed her
clothes, she secreted them in the only place she could
think of: she buttoned them into the front of her riding
habit.

She had tried to be quiet, but was not quiet enough.
As she stole back down the stairs and gained the hallway,
Sir Marcus was standing there waiting for her.

"Going out so early, Miss Balinburgh?"

"I took a fancy to the idea of riding before breakfast."

"Do you usually take your exercise so early?"

"Upon occasion." Ellen was surprised at her own skill
at dissemblance.

"Have you chanced to think further upon my proposal of last night?"

Sir Marcus's demeanor was precisely as it had always
been, so how was it that Ellen now sensed menace
behind his words? Was it her imagination? She did not
think so. Her instinct told her to allay his fears as best
she could.

She looked down, doing her best to look demure. "I
have, Sir Marcus. If it please you... I accept."

He smiled. "I am most heartily glad to hear it," he replied. "Perhaps, then, my dear, it would not be inappropriate..." and approaching Ellen, he took her in his embrace.

Ellen tried not to flinch. Even as his face sought hers, his lips met her lips, she was determined that she would show no sign of disgust. She allowed him to press her towards himself—his embrace tightened—and was interrupted by the rustle of papers in her bodice!

Even then, all might have been well, but Ellen felt herself stiffen with shock, and Sir Marcus felt it too. "What is this?" he asked, releasing her. He glanced at her lapels.

Ellen too looked down. It was barely visible, but she could see it: the corner of the will poking up above the reveres of her riding jacket!

She gasped and pulled away, but Sir Marcus had grasped her wrist. "There is something you wish to hide from me?"

But it seemed that Sir Marcus could not quite bring himself to so abandon decorum as to retrieve the letter himself. "Remove it," he said, the menace in his voice now unmistakable.

Desperately, Ellen shook her head.

"I give you one last chance, Miss Balinburgh," he said. "Let me have whatever it is you have hidden in your bodice!"

But Ellen's attention was fixed at a point behind Sir Marcus's back, for she could see what he could not.

It was a calm, still day. The hallway was never a draughty place, even in the most unsettled of weathers, and moreover, no window was open. Yet, clearly visible to Ellen, the chrysanthemums in their vase on the jardinière were shaking and swaying as if in the strongest of breezes!

It was at this moment that Sir Marcus, losing patience, launched himself at Ellen with a snarl. Ellen started back, but Sir Marcus was upon her, one hand at her breast, tearing off the top button of her jacket, the other closing upon her wrist with a grasp that felt like forged iron!

He had her in his grip, she could not escape, but to Ellen's astonishment, he paused in his attack. His face worked, he seemed to be in some discomfort, his hand fell away from her breast and went to his face—and once again his body convulsed in the throes of a sneeze!

His grasp loosened—it was all that Ellen needed. She broke away from his grip and she ran as fast as her skirts would allow for the front door. To her very great relief old Amos was already there, with the bay mare saddled and bridled and waiting for her next to the mounting block!

Somehow she scrambled into the saddle, and gave a flick of her cane. The mare shied, not recognizing the rider. Ellen lurched in her seat, but the animal settled and started off willingly enough. Behind her she could hear Sir Marcus calling for his horse; the fact that his animal had not been saddled would give her some ground. Gaining the lane, Ellen urged the mare into a smart trot. For a moment she was nearly thrown by the motion, before she found the beast's rhythm and matched it with her own.

It was quite a new thing, riding Constance's mare. She was much further from the ground than when on the gray pony, and the latent power of the animal beneath her disturbed her. Very soon, however, they were making their way up into the hills, and gaining a patch of open country, she found within herself the courage to urge the mare to a canter.

It was as well she did, for looking behind her, she spied Sir Marcus on his own hunter entering the field. How had he followed her so quickly? A glance showed her: he had waited only for the bridle to be put on the animal, and rode bareback, yet despite this he showed no alarm in urging his beast to a gallop! She must escape him, she knew it, and yet she was forestalled by her own fear: she dared not push her own horse to match the other's pace.

She urged the mare as fast as she dared, but inexorably Sir Marcus was gaining on her. And now a new peril was upon her, for she was nearing the top of the field, her path was blocked by a long, low hedgerow, and she could see no gate!

Constance had been used to ride to hounds, and was an intrepid and experienced horsewoman. It had been the cause of uncounted horrors for the more timid Ellen, to imagine her leaping fences and ditches, without even the dubious security of a man's astride seat. In vain had she recounted the tales she had heard of ladies thrown from the sidesaddle and dragged behind the horse to their deaths. Constance would not be deterred.

The horse had been Constance's horse. Even with an inexperienced rider, she had no more fear of the obstacle ahead than her mistress had ever had. She held steady for the hedgerow. Ellen looked behind her, although in truth there was no need: the sound of hooves told her that Sir Marcus was almost upon her.

She looked forward again. The hedgerow was close at hand! Ellen came within a fraction of an inch of abandoning her escape and bringing the horse around, but even as she thought it, she realized it was too late! The mare had committed herself to the action: all Ellen could do was to try to remember everything she had been taught about balance, and close her eyes.

She felt the muscles of the mare bunch beneath her. Her stomach felt as if it had been left beneath them, there was a moment, a split second, in which it felt as if she and the horse were completely still, and then there was a thud, and a jolt, and they were over, and Ellen— miraculously—had kept her seat!

Sir Marcus was still gaining, however. Ellen risked another look behind. He too was urging his horse to the hedge. And then there was a harsh cry and a frantic whir of wings, and a pheasant burst upwards from the hedge-row right into the path of the horse—even as the animal was gathering itself to take the obstacle! The horse shied, using its front legs to push itself abruptly sideways—Sir Marcus's body continued its forward momentum towards the hedge—then Ellen could see him no more, and there was only the riderless hunter, cantering back down the hill, reins flapping loose against its neck.

Ellen could not restrain a cry of triumph. She had not known she had had it in her: never in her wildest dreams could she have imagined herself in a desperate chase, taking hedgerows in her stride! She drove the horse on to a gallop, laughing with delight.

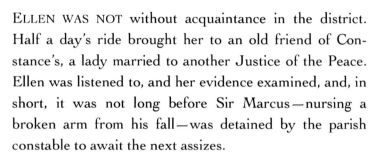

ELLEN WAS NOT without acquaintance in the district. Half a day's ride brought her to an old friend of Constance's, a lady married to another Justice of the Peace. Ellen was listened to, and her evidence examined, and, in short, it was not long before Sir Marcus—nursing a broken arm from his fall—was detained by the parish constable to await the next assizes.

In the meantime the contents of Constance's will were read and honored, and before very much time had elapsed Ellen found herself returned to Constance's house, but this time established as its mistress!

THERE HAD BEEN much to do, when Ellen returned home. The funeral had still to be arranged, the servants instructed, and calls to be made. It was some days before Ellen had the leisure to see to her own business. Eventually, however, her time was no longer so pressed, and she was able to make her way to the library to do what she felt she had to do.

She gathered her writing materials, then sat for a moment, gazing into empty air. There was much that she wished to say, and she must gather her thoughts in order to be able to say it.

My dearest Constance, she wrote...

How could I have doubted you? And yet, when you left me so alone, and although I knew it was not your choice to die, I was so angry with you!

These past five years spent in your house have been the happiest of my life. After I realized that I would never be able to bring myself to marry, I thought that I was fated to live out my allotted years as a humble dependent, never knowing the sweet joys of independence or love. You changed all of that for me. Little did those who knew us as employer and companion realize that the bonds that drew us together were far sweeter and far stronger...

When you died, all of that — love, protection, ease — was snatched away. Can you forgive me for such a betrayal of your memory, for almost succumbing to a loveless marriage for the sake of security and comfort?

I should have known that you would still be there watching over me: that a love like ours could not be cast asunder by mere death. You have left me this dear house, and a competence equal to it, and for that I thank you. And yet, dare I believe there is something more? For I do not understand how it was that my eye was led to the book in your library of which I had the greatest need, and no more do I understand how it was that I was led to find the papers in your drawer, or how the flowers were agitated in the hall, or even how the bird came to be scared from the hedgerow and to startle Sir Marcus's hunter. These things remain a mystery, and I cannot believe they were coincidences.

A tear was running down Ellen's cheek. She paused to wipe it away. Her eyes fell upon the bowl of crimson roses that stood next to her paper. And then, as she watched, a single rose petal gently detached itself from one of the flowers and fell, landing with soft precision next to the most recent sentence Ellen had written.

Ellen drew in her breath. She did not understand— she could only see and believe. Her Constance was constant to her still.

How close Ellen had come to dying herself, that night in the bedchamber! Had she been only a few moments faster in retiring to their bed, she might have joined Constance in death. And yet, despite her grief, despite the loss of the one who meant most to her in all the world, she had never felt so fiercely alive. She had been taught so much in the last few days—she had learned courage and independence, and she would never again, she vowed, put herself in the power of another in return for comfort or protection. In dying, Constance had taught her how to live.

MAJESTIC-12

by
Gay Toltl Kinman

October 1973

IT ALL STARTED with a telephone call from a man named Wilbur, in Roswell, New Mexico.

Professor Sidney Firth's office at UC Berkeley was like all the others in his building: crammed bookcases with no need for bookends, piles of books, loose papers, files on the floor. He had the regulation coatrack, two wooden chairs in front of an old wooden desk and a swivel chair that squealed. The middle drawer of his desk stuck — a symbol of his life.

If only he could get proof.

Then the phone call.

Wilbur took a while to get to the heart of his call.

"Yeah, like he remembers his grandfather telling him about it," Wilbur said.

"What did his grandfather say?"

"That he was out at San Agustin with the Andersons and he had his Brownie with him and took a bunch of pictures. Nobody knew he was doing it."

Wilbur was saying all the right things. Sidney stared out of his window as his pulse began to race. The Andersons had actually seen and described the aliens. One alien had still been alive. What happened after the Army got there, no one knew, and no one was allowed to talk about anything. Could there actually be pictures of the aliens? Then reality brought his hopes back as he tried to pull out the stuck middle drawer to get a pen.

"You mean, there were several people there and no one saw him taking pictures? Those Brownie box cameras were big."

"He told Davey he kinda covered the camera up. Besides, everybody was going too crazy to notice what he was doing."

"But didn't they remember that he had a camera?"

"You want me to tell you the rest of it or not?"

"Yes, yes, of course, please go on."

"Well, like I said, his grandfather's going around taking pictures of the spaceship, and those critters that's on it. Or was on it."

"He has pictures of the aliens?"

"Yep, that's what Davey told me."

"Where are they? Why hasn't anybody seen them?"

"Which question do you want me to answer?"

"Where are the pictures?"

"They're still in the camera, leastwise that's what Davey told me."

"They're still in the camera? Since 1947?"

"That's what Davey told me."

"Why weren't they developed?"

"'Cuz the Army was all over everybody like june bugs on strawberries. Throwing people in jail for a week, scaring citizens, causing all kinds of ruckus. He thought he'd wait 'til the sand settled a little. See which way the wind blew after that. Army was threatening to put some people in an insane asylum outta state. And it wasn't only the Army. Lotsa folk around here thought some people had gone plum crazy. Not only that, they didn't want a bunch of outsiders swarming around. Anyhow, he had the fear o' God in him, that's what Davey told me."

"I'd like to develop those pictures for my book," Sidney said.

"Thought you might. That's why I'm calling. Heard you give that talk here in Roswell a month ago, how you're writing the book and all. Thought you're the right person to get this information. Maybe you'll put my name in your book, something like that?"

"You haven't mentioned this to anyone else?"

"Davey's jist up and told me about it. He's talked about it before but I didn't pay much attention and he really didn't go into any details. Think he was worried about people wanting to send him to some asylum."

"I'd like to interview Davey."

"Well, that's not too possible, seeing as he up and died on me, and I might be going too, soon, so somebody's got to know."

"I've very pleased you contacted me. Having those pictures will prove once and for all the validity of the ideas of a spaceship landing and the existence of life on other planets."

"Don't know about that but it sure will tell everyone that something really happened in St. Agustin."

Sidney's hopes rose again. He'd had many crank calls about Roswell. Not many knew about San Agustin. Yes, Wilbur was saying all the right things.

"St. Agustin and Roswell," Sidney said. "Now, where is the camera?"

"Well, now, that brings me to another part of the problem."

Sidney sighed. His hopes went down. "Let's hear it."

"Davey's grandfather hid the camera 'cuz the Army came out searching his place 'cuz he was with the Andersons. Even dug up his garden because they thought he had some of that material from the spaceship. That metallic stuff. But he swore to them he didn't take any. Didn't matter to the Army, the FBI, and all them other alphabets, they still searched everywhere."

"They didn't find the camera?"

"No, sirree."

"So where is it?"

"Like I said, that's the problem. Davey never did find it."

"Davey didn't find it, but you did?"

"Not exactly. See, his grandfather left a riddle to where the camera was. Leastwise, that's what Davey thought."

"Davey thought his grandfather left a riddle?"

"He was pretty sure. But not like one hundred per cent sure."

Sidney's hopes sank. So tantalizing, but this was going to turn out to be another wild goose chase. Film in a camera. Even if it existed, would it be any good after all this time?

But still Sidney kept on. "All right, we have a riddle from Davey's grandfather. Do you have the riddle?"

"Yessiree, I do."

"Do you have any idea what it means?"

"No siree. If I did, I'd'a found that there camera, had the film developed, and sold it to NBC or CBS for big bucks."

"And you're willing to give it to me for a mere mention of your name in my book?" Sidney could hear the doubt taint his words.

"Well, sir, not exactly. Thought you might give me what's called a finder's fee."

Ah, Sidney sighed again. Just like most of the other callers. "How much do you want?" No doubt in his voice this time, just sarcasm.

"I was thinking in the range of ten thousand."

"What! Ten thousand? Dollars?"

"Of course, dollars. But we can negotiate."

"Negotiate! I could barely give you ten thousand cents."

"I need some money outta this. My Social Security doesn't go too far, and there's a few things I need to do. Like I said, I'm going to be joining Davey up there soon. I got bad lungs and that's what did him in."

Sidney was thinking. He looked out of his window at the building next door, and at a sliver of the campus he could see. He fiddled with the pen he had found under the papers on his desk, the drawer still part way opened, or part way closed, however he wanted to look at it. That decided him. He had to take the chance and not be stuck here like the drawer. He wanted proof beyond a doubt...

"Let me see what I can do. I can draw you up a contract and if everything turns out as you say, I'm sure I can raise some money to pay you. But it would have to be after we produce the evidence."

Sidney imagined from the silence that followed that Wilbur was thinking this over, just as Sidney had. Finally Wilbur said, "Okay, give me one of them there contracts, then that'll have to do."

After they made arrangements to meet, Sidney hung up the phone, feeling hopeful. There'd been other callers willing to show him all kinds of things, including pieces from the spaceship. But Sidney had already seen so many fakes. At the same time, if they could crack the riddle, it sounded like there would be actual photographic proof of a landing. Not that Sidney needed proof to bolster his own belief, but he was a serious researcher. He wanted solid evidence that would prove the truth to the world. This was his life. He believed.

He blocked out time on his calendar for a trip back to Roswell to see Wilbur. Wilbur had said he'd heard Sidney speak in Roswell a month before. Sidney wondered if he had seen him. The place had been packed, but afterwards people had come up to him telling anecdotes from their past about the Roswell incident. There had been one older man loitering on the fringe of the group — overalls, skinny as the proverbial rail, desert-dried skin, chewing on tobacco — had that been him?

The back of Sidney's neck had prickled during their conversation. Everyone talked about Roswell — that was where the Army press release reported picking up a large, disc-shaped flying object from outer space — but San Agustin was where the spaceship had finally ended up.

Sidney had always felt sure someone had taken photographs. Seemed to be the natural thing to do under the circumstances. But before now, he hadn't heard so much as a whisper of it. And now he might get hold of the camera. If it existed.

WHEN SIDNEY REACHED ROSWELL, he checked into the Serendipity Motel. It was an old place, but clean and neat. Maple furniture, a single bed under the front window, and a nightstand with a wagon-wheel-motif lamp. It was exactly like the room he'd stayed in a month earlier, when he'd come here to give his speech.

The next morning, he looked over his papers on the desk, picked up his notes from his telephone conversation with Wilbur, and headed to Mom's Kitchen next door for breakfast. It was 7:30, and only one booth was empty.

He saw Sheriff Barney sitting in the last booth, a folded newspaper spread out next to his plate of fried eggs, ham, and fried potatoes with a stack of toast beside it. The man was a few inches over six feet, and lean. The lower part of his face was tanned, but his forehead, protected by his Stetson, was pale. The hat sat on the seat of the booth, as though to discourage anyone from sitting down in the opposite seat. Sidney had interviewed the sheriff on a previous visit to Roswell. The sheriff didn't look up, so Sidney didn't wave or nod a greeting. And he wasn't about to disturb him.

While eating, Sidney went over his notes and the questions he had jotted down to ask Wilbur. His anticipation level was so high he felt like he was being lifted off the ground. When he was done, the sheriff's plate was gone, but the man was still engrossed in the newspaper.

Sidney paid his bill then walked out to his car. There was a motorcycle parked in front of it, touching his bumper. It looked oversized and mean —just like the man standing next to it. Sidney's heart began to pound again, but not from exhilaration.

"You're that UFO investigator," the man said.

The man had the biggest stomach Sidney had ever seen. The rest of him looked big and solid. One faint word on his tee-shirt curved over the top of his belly. Sturgis.

Sidney swallowed hard. "I investigate claims of extra-terrestrial life."

"You ain't gonna find any of that around here. All that stuff you hear is all made up by crazy people." He whirled a finger in concentric circles next to his head.

Standing farther back was this man's physical oppo-site—tall, thin, with a cadaverous face. Strapped to his back was something like a leather quiver. Sidney recog-nized it as a rifle case.

"Lotsa folks around here don't want Roswell men-tioned in the same breath as those loony UFOer tree huggers. So you might just as well mosey on out of town."

Sidney felt perspiration trickle down from his bald head. Was this man threatening him? Why? What had Wilbur said about some people not happy about Roswell being overrun by strangers? Would the thought actually drive someone to violence? Looking at Mr. Sturgis, it certainly seemed possible.

"Alls I'm saying, Mister Investigator," Sturgis con-tinued, "is that you're done here. Time to move on. Forget you ever heard of them UFOs and leave us alone. Investigate someplace else."

Sidney stuttered something unintelligible, fear having robbed him of control of his voice and tongue.

"Is there a problem here, Professor Firth?"

Sidney nearly cried out in relief when he saw the sheriff striding toward them.

He opened his mouth only to utter another croak.

"No problem," Sturgis replied quickly. "Man here was telling me how he was just this minute leaving town."

"Was he now? We're mighty happy to have visitors stay as long as they like. So maybe you'd better let the gentleman go on with his business, Zeke." The sheriff's Stetson shadowed his face, covering his white forehead. He fingered his gun belt and casually twirled a toothpick in his mouth.

Zeke looked around, trying to be just as casual and said, "Guess I'll be gettin' along."

He climbed aboard his hog with more agility than Sidney would have expected for a man of his size. The thin man climbed on behind him. Zeke gunned the engine a little too long, as though for emphasis, and roared away, cutting off a small truck that honked its horn in aggravated protest.

"Sorry about that," the sheriff said. "In case you didn't know, there's an element here that would like to take the town back in time to before it became a tourist attraction. This UFO stuff has put them over the edge because they don't understand it. If it goes away, then they don't have to deal with it."

Sidney nodded, his mouth dry, eggs, hash browns, buttered toast making a greasy swirl in his stomach. "Thank you, sheriff," he managed to say.

"Others'd be happy to make money any way they can," he continued as if he knew about Wilbur's request.

Sidney nodded, feeling his neck bobbing like one of those dolls in the back of a car window.

"Take care now." The sheriff tipped his hat and sauntered off.

WILBUR MET SIDNEY back at his motel room. Sidney recognized him immediately from his earlier talk. I knew it! He thought.

Sidney cleared a space on the desk so there was room for Wilbur to put down his things. Then he pulled up a chair and gestured for Wilbur to do the same. Though it had taken Wilbur some time to get to the point on the phone, in person, he was all business.

"This here's the riddle," Wilbur said, shuffling through his papers until he found it.

Sidney read.

The arms go around.
The water comes up.
A branch is offered.
X marks the spot.

"Are there any windmills around here?" Sidney asked after a few minutes.

Wilbur laughed. "Me and Davey been over that. Nope, no windmills. Not even anyone thinking about putting a windmill up. The closest we could get was a road that has windmill in the name. Windmill Springs.

"But there ain't no trees out there nowhere. No branches of anything. We went up and down the road a couple of times when Davey got serious about finding the camera. And there ain't no x's out there either."

"Was Davey's grandfather an educated man?"

"He was. Hada lotta book learning. Taught at the high school for a while. English, think it was."

"And he left the riddle to Davey?"

"Yep, said something about it being Davey's inheritance. But to tell you the truth, the old guy was getting pretty senile at that point."

"But he wrote the riddle before?"

"Yessiree, he wrote that soon as he buried the camera."

"But he didn't give it to Davey until later?"

"Well, Davey was away at the time since we were both coal mining in West Virginia. Jist before his grandfather got sick, he told Davey to open it up if anything happened to him. He opened the envelope when the old guy was getting gaga. By then it was too late, his grandfather couldn't tell him anything about anything. In fact, he didn't even recognize Davey. Then Davey started to get sick and he wanted to find out what this inheritance thing was all about. And if there was anything to the old man's story. And that's where we're at now."

Sidney read the riddle again. Then, he looked at the detailed county map and traced Windmill Springs Road.

Long road going off into nowhere—Muriette, Igloo, Steppe, Baseline, Letterman, Tularos—all intersected it along the way.

"Have any of the roads changed names since 1947?"

"None changed that I can recall. New ones added, of course."

Sidney went back to the map, looking at the names and the riddle. Branch. Olive branch. Olive for olive branch.

"Nothing named Olive or—"

"Olive? Only Olive I know of is Olive and Ben Cross."

Cross. X marks the spot.

Sidney tried to slow down his breathing.

"No Olive something in relationship to Windmill Springs Road?" Sidney asked.

"Since you put it that way, yeah, there is. Olive and Ben Cross got themselves a little monument 'bout the size of a tombstone right there on that Road."

"Monument?"

"They owned all that property out there, something like a thousand acres, had no children so they gave it to the State for a wilderness area, sure enough it is. The State ain't done nothing about it, let the place rot. House they lived in, barn, all falling down. Government's claiming it for the State 'cuz it's got some of those endangered species like the lily-livered toad or some-thing, and some yellow flower, both of them ain't anyplace else in the world so's—"

"The monument, it's on Windmill Springs Road?"

"Well, isn't that what I jist said?"

The riddle seemed too easy. Why hadn't Davey made the connection? Maybe he'd lived here too long.

"Will you take me out to see it?"

"Well, yessiree I will."

WILBUR HIT THE ground with the pick in a practiced swing. And again. Sidney had directed him to start in front, but it didn't matter where he started—a shovel was no use on the cement-like earth.

Sidney watched, feeling a bit useless. He hadn't done anything athletic in his life and would probably just make things worse. All the same, it was going to take a long time for Wilbur to dig all around the small monument as the pick just made a little dent in the soil each time. Trying to forget that, in addition to being older, Wilbur had also said he was sick, Sidney directed his attention to the inscription on the monument:

Dedicated to Olive and Ben Cross
Generous patrons of this Wilderness area
1933

The date was well before 1947, so it was possible Davey's grandfather had used the site to bury the camera. Hard to tell after all this time.

Sidney wondered how long Wilbur was going to last with his lung disease. Maybe he should have hired someone in town to do the digging. No, better no one else knew what they were doing. Maybe all they were doing was rearranging the desert floor.

An hour later, Wilbur was still swinging away, albeit much slower, bent over, saying, "Well, lookee here—"

Suddenly, Sidney heard a wet whump. Wilbur sank in slow motion to the ground. The back of his head had a wet spot. A red wet spot. At the same moment, Sidney's knees gave way, having more sense than his brain, and he fell to the ground as a second shot sounded, and a sliver of marble disappeared from the top of the marker.

Sidney rolled toward the monument, taking cover in its pitifully inadequate shade. He looked around but saw no one. Who was shooting at them? And why?

A picture flashed in his mind: the tall, thin, cadaverous-looking man with the rifle case, in the parking lot of the diner.

He lay, curled, against the face of the monument not daring to move. He wanted to run to his car and drive away. Unfortunately, the car was on the other side of the graveled two-lane road. If the sniper was still there, he'd never make it even to the road.

He lay there frozen in place, but baking in the heat. He was wearing a long sleeve shirt and a hat, and was in the shade for now, but that wouldn't last long. When the sun was straight up, the shade would disappear.

He had no idea what to do. Would the sniper wait to see if anyone moved? Would he come down to check on his handiwork? Where was he hiding?

The heat made him dizzy. He was so thirsty, he had to have a drink. He unscrewed the cup from the thermos, took the top off, and drank. He could only swallow a mouthful before he choked, coughed. He waited and tried to relax, letting just a trickle of water down his throat, then another.

His right leg was tingling with pins and needles. He had to move. He looked at his watch. It seemed like he'd been there all day. But the sniper could wait as long as he could. Presumably the sniper had shelter, water, food, was used to the terrain, and knew how to survive. The sniper could easily outwait him.

He decided to take his chances. He wanted to find out what Wilbur had seen before he was shot. Peeking out from behind the monument, he still didn't see anyone. Emboldened, he scuttled over to where Wilbur lay and took the pick out of the poor dead man's hand. His heart pounding, he started to dig where Wilbur had left off, expecting another shot at any moment.

Then the pick struck something hard. Harder than the sun-baked earth.

A metal box.

Sidney dug harder, faster, working to unearth the box.

The box had a handle on the top. He struggled to pull the box out of its resting place. Then he used the pick to pry open the rusted lid.

Inside, something was wrapped in some kind of cloth.

He unwrapped a corner of it and glimpsed a part of the Brownie box camera.

Dizzy with the prospect of what he had found, he pushed the dirt back into the hole with the end of the pick. Lordy, it was hot. Maybe the sniper was waiting to see what he'd dug up. Maybe the sniper had just been waiting for Sidney to do the hard work.

Suddenly a motor sounded in the distance.

Staggering to his feet, the box under his arm, Sidney tried to run across the road to his car. His right leg was completely numb, and his legs were too unsteady; he scrabbled along crabwise instead. He opened the door, put the box behind his seat and crawled in.

And then he saw the flashing lights behind him. He heaved a sigh of relief. The sheriff had saved him once. This would make twice.

Unless the sheriff was the sniper.

Sidney's hands were shaking so badly, he dropped the keys. He watched, pulse racing as the sheriff's car turned, then stopped in front of the monument.

Sidney bent over, groping for the keys.

He heard the sheriff slam the car door, his feet scraping on the gravel as he walked over to Wilbur's body. The sheriff looked up, pulling the brim of his hat lower to shade his eyes, and surveyed the landscape.

Then Sidney saw him fix his eyes on Sidney in the car.

Sidney stuck the key in the ignition and turned it.

Click, click.

He tried again.

The sheriff started across the road toward him. There was no escape now. Sidney searched for some sign that would tell him if the sheriff was a good guy or a bad guy.

He still couldn't tell as the sheriff met his eyes.

"Figured Zeke and his friend might follow you two. Wilbur was prancing around like he had a big secret. Let people know he was coming into some money. So I followed Zeke, not hard to track on a dusty road with the way he was riding. Knew he was up to something. What did old Wilbur promise you anyway?" He glanced at the box on the floor behind Sidney.

Sidney felt as though he couldn't move. In a quavery voice, he answered, "He said something was buried out here. Wanted me to see it. Pay him if it turned out to be something of importance."

"What did he say it was?"

Sidney looked at the sheriff. He was in the middle of the desert with a dead man and a dead battery. Soon he might be joining them. Sidney didn't lie well, and he knew the sheriff wouldn't believe him if he did. He just shook his head.

The sheriff huffed, but he didn't press the issue. "Look, I know you didn't kill old Wilbur. I saw Zeke and his friend running away from here like two bats out of hell. My deputy has probably already picked them up. As for you…"

Sidney went cold, even though the temperature was still hot.

"… I've got some jumper cables in the trunk so I can give you a start. You go back to the motel. I'll come over as soon as I can to take your statement. Don't even think about leaving town until then, though."

"No, sir, I won't." Sidney heard his own voice, as shaky as he was.

He had the camera. He had the camera! And he'd found a man in Roswell who claimed he could bring up an image on old film. His heart pounded like a young man in love, the danger of the past hours forgotten.

SEVERAL HOURS LATER—he had been aware of every minute as he waited in his motel room—Sidney looked at the photos, disappointment making him sag. His photo specialist had done his best, but the pictures all had a light streak down the left side like a lightning bolt. Two of the pictures showed a pair of kids pointing at something, while kneeling beside something that looked like it had four long fingers. But it could have been just a shadow. Or a dead branch. People in the other pictures looked ghostly, but recognizable. Not aliens. No spaceship.

Wilbur had said Davey's grandfather had used something to conceal the camera. Was that what was over the lens? Were the aliens, like vampires, not photogenic? Had the film been old when it was put into the camera? Had there been a light leak in the old Brownie?

Sidney would never know. He'd have a real specialist in Berkeley look at the pictures, but he felt even with his expertise, there'd be no conclusive proof.

He went back to his room, sat on the sagging bed holding the pictures, almost wanting to throw them into the dented wastepaper basket. So close…

And then it hit him.

The rusted metal box.

He'd been so fixated on the camera that he hadn't paid too much attention to what it was wrapped in. He opened the box again. Some kind of oilcloth, thick. As he examined it, he realized it was two layers sealed together. The glue around the edges was coming unstuck. He began to pull it apart.

His heart pounded.

Between the layers was another piece of material— unwrinkled, shiny, its edges cut. It was thin, giving forth a slight crinkly sound.

This was the real prize not the pictures.

It was fabric from the spaceship. It had to be. The ship the government had said at first had landed, then denied.

Conclusive proof for his book. He'd done it! He had the proof! He almost did a little dance, but halted in mid-step.

Outside was the rumble of a motorcycle engine.

Then a knock at his door.

Sidney's heart thumped, surely loud enough to be heard by whoever was at the door.

Oh, God! No.

It was Zeke and the rifleman come to kill him and take the evidence. But how? Hadn't the sheriff's deputy arrested them? Were they released already?

Whimpering in his fright, he shoved the box under the bed.

"Open up, professor. I know you're in there."

It wasn't Zeke's voice. Was it the rifleman?

"Hey, I saved your life. Open up. We can make a deal."

The doorknob rattled and the door opened.

Good God, he'd forgotten to lock it. The rifleman strode in.

"Thing is," he said, looking around the small room, "my friend Zeke, he just doesn't want people to write about Roswell. He's an Army man, so whatever the

Army said was right. A weather balloon? Yep, that's what it was."

Sidney stood up on shaky legs and moved to the desk chair. He dropped into it. The man stood, framed in the doorway, the rifle case over his shoulder.

"Me, I think there's a little money to be made here. Saw you found something. Guess you were going to pay old Wilbur a few bucks. Since he isn't around to collect, why not give it to me? The money and whatever you found."

Sidney cleared his dry throat. "Wasn't going to give him anything until after the book was published. I don't have any money to speak of."

"Then give me what you dug up. I told Zeke to let you two do the dirty work. Then he could get rid of it if he wanted to. I didn't expect you to find anything. But when you did, well, I knew I wasn't going to let Zeke get rid of it."

"Where is Zeke?" Sidney could see the motorcycle outside.

Ignoring the question, the rifleman continued. "He was just taking potshots at you both to scare you off, only he's not a good shot. Took my gun while I was off having a piss. Should never have left it on the bike. Anyhow, you can go or stay, as you please, all I want is what you found."

Sidney's mind was racing. "Pic... pictures. But they're not very good. Here. Have a look." Sidney spread the photos out on the desk.

The man glanced at them, then scooped them up and made for the door.

Then stopped.

The sheriff appeared on the other side, his gun already in hand. "I'll take that rifle, Bradley."

"It was Zeke who shot him! Said he just wanted to scare them off!" Bradley was talking fast. Sidney thought he sounded nervous.

"The rifle," the sheriff said again.

Bradley started to stuff the pictures into his pocket.

"And those pictures."

Sidney could tell Bradley wasn't happy about that. He looked like he was deciding what to do. But the rifle was in its case, and the sheriff just clicked off the safety on his. At least, that's what Sidney took that sound to be.

"Put them on the bed. Nice and easy."

Bradley did as he was told.

"Now, you and your friend may have slipped past my deputy earlier, but he caught up with Zeke, and now we can all go over to the station and find out what really happened out there."

The deputy came in and Sidney saw his hand close around Bradley's arm to lead Bradley outside.

The sheriff moved the pictures around on the bed with the barrel of his gun, looking at them.

Sidney didn't move. His heart was jumping out of his chest and his hands and feet felt like ice, yet sweat dripped down his face.

"Not much good. Like the ones of Nessie in Scotland, or those ones Conan Doyle took of the fairies."

Sidney was surprised that the sheriff could make those references. He hadn't struck Sidney as a particularly educated man when Sidney had interviewed him the previous month.

The sheriff continued. "Best you leave now, Dr. Firth. We'll sort out who really fired the rifle and killed Wilbur. Suspect it's as he said. Don't think Zeke wanted to kill anyone. He's all talk, mostly. Gets in a bar fight once in a while. Bradley might have though, if he wanted the goods bad enough." He picked up the pictures. "I'll take these. Have a nice evening, professor." The sheriff walked to the door, and, with one final glance at Sidney, pulled it closed.

Sidney sat like a statue. He felt as though he was made of cement, stone, marble, whatever made up a statue. He barely breathed. He took stock of where he was with his book. The pictures and the story of Wilbur and Davy's grandfather would have been a very interesting inclusion. But without the pictures, inconclusive as they were, that story was dead.

He still had the cloth in the tin box under the bed. He glanced over and saw that the bedspread didn't completely cover it. The door wasn't locked.

He had to get up and lock the door.

No, he had to get up and get out of there. He had to move. He went over the steps in his mind—throw everything from the drawers and the closet into his suitcase. He thought about putting the tin box in there also. He didn't want to put it in his suitcase, as that would be the first place someone would look. He was getting paranoid. Just get up, he told himself, get everything, put it in the car, and drive away.

Inertia, but he knew it had to be shock. Shock at seeing someone shot in front of his eyes. Elation at the
pictures, then deflation when they were not usable. He
had to move. But he felt like he had been drugged. The
fabric—that was his salvation. That's what he should live
for. So why couldn't he move? The sheriff had told him
to leave. What was wrong?

All of a sudden, a pain like a lightning bolt shot
through his brain.

No!

He suddenly felt paralyzed and numb.

Oh, God! Was he having a stroke?

He had to get an aspirin. There was a little box in his
pants' pocket....

He tried to stand, but his legs gave out. He felt himself crumple, in slow motion, to the floor. He was aware
of what was happening, but couldn't move. Then everything went blank.

"AHHGG," Sidney said. The tin box.

"You're awake. That's wonderful. The doctor will be
here in a few minutes. You've had a stroke. Are you
comfortable? Is there anything I can get you?"

Sidney could hear what the nurse was saying, but
without his glasses, she was just a blur. He was in a
white, brightly lit room—that much he could tell. In a
bed with metal rails. A hospital bed.

"Ahhgg." *The tin box.*

"Don't worry. With therapy, your speech will likely
return. Just relax. You're in good hands here. Don't

worry about your things. The hotel has packed them up and put them in your car. They'll keep your car in the lot as long as you need it to be there."

"Ahhgg." *The tin box.*

"Just relax, the doctor will be here soon. He's making his rounds. It's wonderful you're awake."

"Ahhgg…"

ROSA ENTERED THE motel room. She knew the guest had been taken away in an ambulance. At least he hadn't died in the room. No, she wasn't superstitious, but she didn't want to go into a room where someone had died.

There was nothing of his there, and it was as though he had moved out on his own. She pulled off the bedspread and draped it over the desk chair, then she pulled off the sheets and remade the bed. Her assistant was cleaning the bathroom. Rosa dusted and began to vacuum. As she ran the machine beside the bed, she heard a clunk. It had hit something. She turned off the vacuum and bent down to look under the bed.

A tin box.

How long had it been there?

She knew the maid before her had been fired for not doing a thorough job, so she wasn't surprised that something would be under the bed that hadn't been moved.

She pulled it out. Rusty. Ugh. She should just throw it away. Then she looked closer. Maybe her uncle Rito could clean it up. If so, it could be used for something. She sat there on her haunches for a few moments looking at the box, then she stood and opened it up. A clump of something. She dumped it into the trash canister and put the box on her cleaning cart.

She looked around. Everything was ready for the next guest. She closed the door.

JUANITA AND THE CAVE OF THE WINDS

by
Leonhard August

THERE'S A PLACE in the mountains and desert that is our home, that hardly anyone talks about—except when they want to scare kids and give them a lesson in wanting too much for themselves. I know it's real. I've been there and, thanks to the teaching good people gave me along the way, I made it back.

I'm not anybody special. I had ideas at one time or another that I could be a world-beater in one thing or another, but that was when I was young and I hadn't figured out that you don't have to be the best to be the best you can be. Being happy with yourself is something we're okay with to a point, but pride goeth before a fall was part of our way of life before it was written in the Bible.

I'm a good hand with a rope at round-up time. I'm a decent shot with pistol or long gun. I'm a little better parent than most, but that's because my kids are a lot better than most. I'm a good enough police officer that the Tribe, the Tohono O'odham Nation, made me a detective in the TOPD. I've reached what should be the middle part of my life. God willing, I'll have 30 years more to get to Elder status, when again, Jiosh willing, I can reflect and regret at leisure. From this vista, though, I think that the regrets will be small and personal. I faced some tough choices, and I haven't screwed up bad as yet. Here's one of the things I mean.

The Cave of the Winds is about dreams. Not the good kind of dreams that guide you and motivate you, but selfish, all-consuming dreams. The kind that won't let you say "good enough" or let you drop them before you hurt yourself or someone else.

OUR HIMDAG, our traditional and cultural foundation, is full of wisdom. Part of that wisdom is to recognize the difference between hopes, dreams, plans, and obsession. Part of our cultural teaching identifies points of crisis in peoples' lives, and instructs us on how to deal with them based on our shared experience. Some of the teachings in our Himdag have to do with relationships between our world and the Spirit World.

To us, each place in our land has a natural relationship to the world we see, and to the unseen world. This coexistence of Worlds also means that there are places of significance and places of Power. There is beauty in these special places because there exists both a harmony and a tension. There are locations where the two worlds touch and Spirits mingle with the living. Sometimes there is danger in these places – both physical danger and even more serious danger. Those places and those who dwell there can harm you or those you love.

The O'odham have been here in the Southwest— southern Arizona, California, and northern Mexico—for thousands of years, and during that time much in our environment has changed. The coming of the Jujkam from the south, and later, the coming of the Medigan from the east, meant that our ways had to change if we were to survive. The underlying wisdom of our Himdag, though, is timeless and unchanging. Regardless of the way the world has turned, the choices that each genera- tion faces have stayed the same: the choice between "me" and "we." The choice between "as much as I want" and "as much as is good." There are no fixed answers, but there are clues that we learn from our elders and our family.

I met Juanita at Pima Community College in Tucson. I had finished my tour in the service, and was getting ready to apply to the TOPD. I was studying law enforcement, with an eye to entering the police academy. She was getting her credits in order so that she could apply to the University of Arizona; she wanted a degree in public administration. Even in those days, I guess, you could call her "driven."

Her family owned a place in town, and when they found out I was commuting to Tucson from the Res, they let me stay in their guest house until I finished the academy. They received some "propers" for doing something nice for a Homeboy, and on my part, I was clean, from a community not too far from theirs, and had prospects of getting a good job. It worked out well for me because I could use the gas money I saved to take their daughter out on Saturday nights.

Juanita's Dad was from a big ranching family on the eastern side of the Res, but he had long ago left that life behind for academia. He taught O'odham culture and language at Pima and the University of Arizona. He had a national reputation among Native American organizations as a poet, singer, and storyteller. Whenever there was a National Meeting or Regional Gathering or Testimonial Dinner in Indian Country, he would be invited to be keynote speaker, color commentator, or MC. He was always in demand and always introduced as "The World's Foremost" or "Greatest" whatever. You know his name. To me he will always be "her Dad" or just "Dad." I lived with them for two years, and they were like my adopted family by the time our paths parted.

Juanita's mother never felt the need to compete. She was a basket maker, and her art was her life. She gathered or grew the traditional materials, then lovingly prepared them and created the finished basket. She knew the traditional patterns and techniques and she had learned the generations of songs and stories behind her art from her mother. In turn, she taught the history, skills, and values to all who came to her to learn, including her children. All four of her daughters followed their mother's teaching and example.

Both Mom and Dad grew up with and knew the traditional teachings. They had grown up with Himdag as everyday guidance for daily living. It was given as a gift to them by their parents and grandparents. They must have been aware of the teachings regarding contact between the living and the Spirit World and the dangers that came with it.

It must have been difficult, though, for Mom and Dad to give that knowledge to their daughters. They lived away from our home lands. Grandparents visited infrequently. The topic of the Spirit World seemed even farther away during the family's dinnertime conversations about school and boys. Tales of Spirits and danger hardly ever made it on the menu.

Some of the girls went to college, some didn't. Some of the girls carried on the basket maker tradition as deeply as their mother did, some didn't. Some of the girls married, some didn't. They were happy, for the most part, with their choices.

But not Juanita. She was the youngest sister. I guess she felt she had to compete with everybody for attention and affection. And that included Mom and Dad. Especially Dad. Maybe she thought she was clumsy with the basket maker's tools. Maybe she felt like her sisters were too good for her to compete with. Maybe she thought baskets were just too B-O-R-I-N-G compared to the bright public spotlight her Dad lived in. Maybe she just wanted to make her mark in time and maybe she figured that the best way to do that was to be better than "The Greatest…"

About the time I finished up at ALETA, the Arizona Law Enforcement Training Academy, Juanita graduated from the U with her public administration degree. With her it was highest honors, of course. From there, it was a few short steps to internships in DC. Over time, our congressmen and our senators were very helpful in finding her a place, first on their staff, and then in Federal agencies. When she graduated from Georgetown Law, all of us that were left behind on the Res figured we'd never see her again except every ten years or so at Christmas. We were wrong, though.

She had buddied-up tight with a bunch of Republicans at the Department of Interior—actually, the Bureau of Indian Affairs but BIA's a dirty word in DC. When the Dems were swept into the Executive Office, she was swept out. Which did not sit well with Miss-Perfect-Native-American. Her DC mentors had not taught her how to use the Republican revolving doors between agency desk and lobbying firms, or that DC survival is essentially cannibalistic, as in "They eat their young." There was no loyalty to friends and colleagues in the scramble out the exit door. When she fell from her high horse, she hadn't looked ahead to find a soft place to fall.

Her Godfathers were all very, very sorry, but "There's just no position open for you at the new company." Meaning, "You can't bring paying clients with you to the lobbying firm, so f*** off." With no prospects of work in DC, Juanita shipped her belongings back home to her parents in Tucson. She'd rest up and consult with her Dad about a next move. Maybe her Washington experience could be useful to the Tribe. But coming home from the heights of DC to work on the Tohono O'odham Reservation would be humiliating, unless....

Her whole life, Juanita always aimed high and shot for the top, no matter what. If she could turn her return to the TO Res into a "Triumphant Return to Lead Her People," she would keep her pride. If she could turn it into revenge against the DC crowd that had left her out, well then, that just sweetened the pot. Juanita plotted her triumphant return with her Dad. She had to choose between falling in with the Reservation political establishment and fighting it; between taking a high paid, but powerless, staff position or running for political office; between taking the long road, starting with a minor political office, or going straight for a top spot. Juanita's Dad had faced those choices too as a young man. He had been a much sought-after potential candidate for the Council or for Chairman after he received his PhD. His choice was to reject all of those options. He'd left TO for an off-Reservation career.

Juanita decided to run for the top spot, the Executive Office: Tribal Chairwoman. No starting at the bottom. No preliminaries. She knew that anything else was a dead end. She told her Dad that Chairwoman had a nice ring to it, and the office could accommodate her for the next four years or more. "More importantly, Dad," she expounded, "it will let me prepare for my real objectives. I'll make the statewide and national connections I'll need for my next step. I want to be Senator when Mr. Too-Many-Houses-to-Count is finally too senile to run again. I'll be the 'Indian Who Lifted Up Her People.' I'll be the 'Washington Insider with Down Home Connections.' I'll be the 'Arizona Country Girl Who Can Get Things Done in Washington.' Nobody will be able to stop me."

One day, I'll be the first Native American President of the United States of America. Those bastards that shut me out will have to crawl and kiss my feet when I'm their boss.

Juanita's Dad was keeping something to himself, though, at least for the time being. He wanted to see Juanita make a great leap forward, just as he had. He promised Juanita that he would help her get to the top, and he knew of a way to make that happen. But that way required that she make a choice based upon her own Spirituality and moral compass. "Selling Her Soul" was one way to say it, but the end result was that Dad's way would make even the impossible a sure thing. He would show her how when the time was right.

Primaries are the first order of business for any Chairman/woman candidate. She decided that she'd pitch her candidacy on her strengths. She would run as an outsider, but an outsider whose DC knowledge and connections would be very useful to the Tribe. Throw out the same old candidates who run every election, and put me in! I can Get Things Done! More Federal Dollars! Better Education! Better Border Protection! Jobs! Per Capita Dollar Distributions! But there were two essential deficiencies that she had to address. The Chairman must speak the O'odham language, and the candidate must have community presence.

Unfortunately, Juanita's parents had chosen to live off-Res. Juanita herself had been at the U or in DC for the last 10 years. Her opponents would say, "Where is her connection to the People?" Luckily, like most O'odham, she had no shortage of relatives, and O'odham always believe in blood before politics. When her relations and supporters opened their community resources to Juanita, her problem became too many opportunities rather than too few. She couldn't possibly make all the village and district Council meetings to which she was invited, much less the Feast days, Saturday dances, Sunday Masses, school picnics, parties, and annual remembrance services. Triage of public appearance opportunities boiled down to the calculus of which date promised the most votes. Which district had more voters? Which village had friendlier disposition toward her? Which family would hold a grudge for a snubbed invitation? How fast could her driver go without getting too many tickets?

Since the latter was a problem shared by each of the candidates in the primary, TOPD stepped in to provide escorts to all of the candidates. We were technically "security detail" but everybody knew we were there to hustle the candidates along to their next destination safely and with a minimum of fuss. I was assigned as Juanita's driver because of our previous connection.

And this reunion of sorts was what showed me that the Cave of the Winds wasn't just a scary story meant to keep kids in line.

After an early evening appearance at a particularly rowdy dance in the District of Sif Oidak, Juanita and her Dad asked me to take a side trip. They told me that an old Auntie, who lived nearby, wanted to see Juanita and give her blessing to the campaign. Even though it wasn't late by O'odham standards—all-nighters being our tradition—I felt my back sag against the driver's seat. It'd been a long day already and this meant that I wouldn't see my kids tonight. I sighed at the price I had to pay for rubbing elbows with the "O'odham jet-set." They told me that I could just drop them at her cousin Fred's ranch house, and someone from the family would take them to her Auntie's place, further up the dirt Reservation Road into the mountains. I guess I protested too weakly, because they insisted and said it was settled. I would stay with the G-plate sedan and sleep until they came back, then we'd go back to town. When we got to the ranch, Juanita and her Dad said goodnight to me and walked up to where her cousin sat in his truck.

It was a damn fine tricked-out Toyota 4x4 for a hard-scrabble cattle ranch like this, considering the low price of beef. Raised the hairs on the back of my neck. There's honest ways to come by such a fine truck, and there's the other kind. Me being a detective, of course, I knew that her Cuz didn't have a regular job. That made me down-right curious. On the Res, without a permanent job, high-paying gigs tended to be in the smuggling line: people or contraband. Musicians never made much in cash, and cowboyin' didn't ever pay much more than room and board. This whole setup didn't smell like a midnight visit to Auntie. I wondered what Cuz and Daddy had cooked up for Juanita tonight. If they were meeting campaign contributors, I'd bet that the donors would not want their pictures published in the weekly O'odham Runner newspaper.

They took off on a ranch road that I had used when I worked on round-ups in my younger days. I waited a little while for them to get ahead, letting them think I'd remained behind in the sedan as we'd agreed. Once they'd gotten far enough up the road, I'd borrow one of the ranch horses and follow.

THAT PARTICULAR ROAD stuck out in my mind, because the regular hands had acted kind of funny about it once we'd gotten out of sight of the bunkhouse. Usually, the older men would have some fun green-horning the new guys on the round-up. Bragging, tall tales, the cowboy equivalent of ghost stories around the cook fire were all common ways to ride the kids that were in the bunch before we all collapsed in our bedrolls. But there was none of that on this road.

The memory of the first night on that round-up came directly to mind without my reaching for it.

Even the old men had been kind of jumpy that night. They wanted only to eat, rest, and then get the hell out of there with whatever stray cattle we could find. As for me, I was one of the new, green kids. I'd come from a different part of the Res. I didn't know this area or its stories. They could've had a bunch of fun jerking me around if they'd had the inclination. But that night they held back, way back. Finally, when the silence became too much, I had to ask someone about the mood everyone was in: quiet and skittish, ready to jump at the slightest noise — or no noise at all.

The foreman of our bunch was a Latigo-tough old cowboy by the family name of Counts-the-Days. His family, way back when some time, must've had the responsibility of keeping the calendar stick: important happenings, community records and such, and the ceremonial duties around planting and harvest. He was lean, and bandy-legged from riding too many horses — starting before he could walk, they say. He was mean as a whip and just as ready to snap at you if you didn't pull your weight. He waited a long minute after I asked him why everyone was so quiet, and then he told me about the Cave of the Winds.

He told me that out here on the trail, in the mountains, you are always closer to Nature, and to the Spirits. Our People don't believe in "ghosts" in the same way European folk do. We do know that there are Spirits, and that they are part of the natural world that we all live in. He talked to me kindly, like he was explaining things to a kid from his own family.

"Mainly, the Spirits a cowboy'll run into aren't mean, and they generally don't intend any harm," he told me. "But this trail is different. It's best to keep in a bunch at night and protect yourself with good thoughts and good intentions."

I couldn't believe that Old Mister Whipcrack himself was giving me advice like my Mother's Elder Brother.

"You don't know the story of this place, do you, boy? You're from over the East Side."

In his experience the East Side was a hotbed of People Who Talked Funny, pig-headedness, and downright ignorance. Well, he looked me up and down, and saw that at least the last part was true. I had no idea of why this place was special.

"Hidden at the end of one of these side canyons is the Cave of the Winds," he began. "The Spirits of the Cave of the Winds are powerful. As powerful as any devil or angel they teach you about in Church on Sunday. They are immortal, and they'll be living in that cave when you and me are long gone, maybe until the world wears itself out and the sun dies. And they hate. They hate the world they made for themselves in that cave. They hate the world outside the cave, and they hate people like us that live outside. So much hate spills out of them that it makes this a dangerous place." The old man ended with a wave of his arm to show he meant the whole canyon. By this time the others in our crew had gathered around the foreman and me. Some of the older hands were nodding in agreement. Some of the younger ones looked as scared as I felt.

"But what do they want? How can they hurt us?" I asked him quietly.

"They want us to be like them. Trapped in that cave until the end of time. They'll reach out and try and get you, too," he said—staring right into my eyes to make the point. "They will promise you your heart's desire, and they can deliver. You want to be a Rodeo Champion? They can make it happen. You want to marry the prettiest girl in the community? They can put her in your bed. You want horses? Gold? Done. They are that powerful."

The older cowhands murmured in agreement. Yes, it's true, they said. They had all heard about someone from one community or another that had made a deal with the Spirits of the Cave.

"But what's wrong with that?" the youngest kid in the bunch interrupted.

"Payback," replied the old foreman. "Payback."

One of the other old hands filled in, explaining, "The bargain you make with the Spirits of the Cave is that you will get your heart's desire in this world, but at the end of your time you will return and stay with them forever in that Cave. You must obey them in this life, and in the next."

"When you pass from this life," said another, "you will not go on into the next world. You will remain with them in the Cave of the Winds. They will feed on your sorrow and regret, and they will torment you until you become as crazy as they are. They get their power from destroying those lost souls."

In our culture, this is a tale that is intended to make young people consider their hopes and dreams in a new light. How do you calculate the price of your dreams? Can your greed lead to your destruction? But they were talking about the Cave as if it were a real, physical place. I didn't sleep much that night. I was a lonely teenager out on the round-up, in the middle of nowhere, thinking about those questions. And about their consequences.

I FOUND MYSELF back in the here and now when I heard the noise. I looked up. Up ahead, the Toyota King-Kong bounced its skid plate off a rock that stuck up in the middle of the road, and when it bounced it scraped its side against an old Kui, a mesquite tree. Judging by the scars I'd seen on the vehicle, I guessed it was traditional for Cuz to give that tree a whack with his truck when he went up that road, maybe for luck.

The Cave of the Winds was far from my mind as I got out of the sedan to follow the political Dynamic Duo in their chauffeured Cowboy Cadillac. Tonight would be a different night with different questions. Where was Juanita going with her Dad and her Cuz? Who would I see? What would I see? I knew I had to find out more than they wanted me to know. I always trust people until they show me their bad side, but my money was still against this trip being tea and cookies with Old Auntie Insomniac. Smuggling and human trafficking would not get a pass from me, even if it involved my second, my adopted "family."

I threw a halter on the tamer-looking of two cow ponies that were corralled out back of the bunkhouse, and mounted up bareback. I knew Old Mister Whipsnap,

Counts-the-Days, was too tough to die. He had retired to be head of the TO Cattlemen's Association over in Sells, but his successor probably bunked in there. If someone stuck their head out of the bunkhouse window to ask me what I was doing, I didn't know how I'd have explained it. I just knew I had to follow Juanita up the canyon, whatever her business turned out to be.

It was easy to follow the dust kicked up by the fat tires on the Toyota as it traced the twists and turns of the canyon road, even by moonlight. I held back and kept to the shadows, so they wouldn't see me if they looked back when they crested a ridge. I didn't think the folks in the truck would be looking for a tail; the real reason I held back is so I wouldn't be spotted in case they picked up an escort. They turned off the ranch road onto a round-up trail—two ruts that led up to a run-down corral that was used twice a year for branding calves. They locked the hubs and put the Toyota into 4-wheel drive, then went on past the cattle pen. I put my pony in 4-hoof drive and followed, half hidden in a wash that went up alongside the trail.

This particular side canyon was one I'd not gone up into when I was here as a ranch hand. The passable part of the canyon looked like it dead-ended at a steep cliff at the end of the trail. The cliff face went straight up a couple hundred feet. No self-respecting stray—calf or steer—would go that far up the box canyon looking for forage, so there had been no need for a round-up hand to waste time up there either. The Toyota parked at the base of the cliff, and I'll be danged if all three of the passengers didn't disappear after taking a step or two. I did a double take, shaking my head to clear it, and then I nudged my pony farther up-slope to get a better view of the truck from above.

Tarnation if there wasn't a break in the rock just ahead of it, with a big slab of fallen down rock that sat like a door to the opening. A little light showed around the edges of the slab, bouncing up from some source deep within the mountain. The cave, the rock, and the light had all been hidden from view from below. Unless you saw it from up here, there was nothing showing that would make you think the cliff face was anything but solid.

I nudged my pony again to head closer, but this time she balked—puffing out her cheeks and making that little huffing sound that means No way, pal. I was afraid that if I pushed her harder, she'd put up a fuss, and I didn't want the noise to alert whoever was down there. I didn't know who might be inside the cave, or outside standing watch over the place. I knew it wasn't Auntie, though, and I was darn sure that Juanita, Dad, and Cuz wouldn't welcome me to whatever party was going on. Neither would whoever invited them here.

I crossed my fingers, hoping the pony was trained for drop-rein, and left her untethered while I made my way slowly below. There wasn't anyone keeping watch when I got to the rock door, at least no one that I could see— and believe me, I looked hard. I slipped behind the rock and into the cave mouth, stopping to let my eyes adjust. The interior was lit by a fire at the other end of the room. It wasn't a big room, I guess, by the standards of other southern Arizona caves. I've been to Colossal Cave and

Karchner Caverns. But the way it stretched back into the darkness, I couldn't tell where it ended. It might have gone on a long ways under the mountain.

The room was dry. In cavers' terms, it looked to be "dead" as opposed to "active" and growing. To me, as a non-caver, I thought it had the look of dead, and it had the smell of dead, too. I thought about I'itoi's Ki, the cave near the summit of Wa:w Giwulk, in the Baboquivari Mountains. That's a dry cave too, but when you enter that Ki, it seems alive—alive with the hopes and prayers of O'odham who climb and visit there on a spiritual journey. This fire-lit cave, here at the end of a box canyon, didn't look like it'd seen any hope in a long, long time.

Down at the end of the room, maybe thirty or forty yards away, I saw them. And heard them. Cave acoustics are unpredictable, and it just so happened that there was a hollow in the rock, a niche next to the door that caught every word that was said at the other end. That's where I put my good ear.

A fire burned bright where they all sat. Kind of an odd fire, it was; it gave off light but it didn't give off smoke or heat. You'd think they'd be taking off their jackets or choking on smoke down there so close, but no. They just sat, talking O'odham in the old way.

The old way of speaking is beautiful. Words rich with meaning put into complex verbal constructions with layers of both denotation and connotation. You have to listen close to old folks when they speak like that. They don't talk in a straight line between point A and point B. They talk around issues and topics, and they say what they mean by not saying what they mean until they take a dozen twists and turns between here and there. They put out a bunch of ideas all at once, kick them around, and mess them together. Then they whittle away at the pile until the only thing left is the one thing they really intended to say right from the start. And it's their gift to you. You've had the beauty and experience of looking at all the ideas from different angles and sorting through them while listening.

There were four Elders sitting in the firelight. There were more in back of them – not easy to say how many or what they were like in the half-light where they sat. The Elders were passing the pipe back and forth as they talked. I could smell the burning herb they call Buzzard Smoke, the pipe-weed that's favored by the clan on this side of the Nation. On the other side of the fire sat Juanita. Her Dad and her Cuz were beside her, but somehow it didn't seem like they were with her. I won't try to repeat the discussion that went on that night. It went on for a long time as they carved away the unnecessary and teased out the important stuff.

It woke me up like a slap in the face when I finally realized that all along they had been bargaining. What is it that you want? How do you think we can help? What will you do in return? When will you repay our kindness? Those were the ideas left after all the verbal round-and-round. Juanita did not have the O'odham language—manners or vocabulary—to keep up with the Elders. Her cousin and her Dad translated from Juanita's direct statements in Medigan English into our words. She was far too impatient for the customary old style O'odham manners and speech. Her impatience showed in quick words, direct answers: I want to be Chairwoman, then Senator, then President. If you can't get me there, then I'm out of here.

I blinked then choked at the raw ambition that her words portrayed. No softness. No compromise. She was the center, the center of the Big Picture. Everything else was a detail to be handled by others. You can help me or get out of my way! I am in command! I knew the deal had been done when the Elders began presenting their gifts—language, political allies, recognition. The four Elders bid Juanita to approach them on their side of the cold fire. One of the oldest looking among them laid hands on her. He looked like Rev. Jimmy John Billy Bob on TV gonna-make-the-lame-walk. That's when the singing began. First, it was the old man with his hands on her shoulders. Then the song was taken up by several of the Elders in the background. Then smoke. Then pollen and a Buzzard's wing.

Juanita looked up at the Old Man and began to speak in tongues. Except it was our tongue. Fluent O'odham in the old style. The words were soft and comforting—persuasive, not like the spoiled child that demanded help-me-or-get-out-of-my-way.

"God will reward you, my precious Elders for your generous assistance to a poor female who seeks only to move forward enough to help the People...." You get the idea.

Their spokesman, their "Big Man," said, "You will also have the support of all of those who are indebted to us. They are many. There are those who have promised themselves, and there are many others who they have pledged to bring to us. We will instruct them that your mission and success are necessary as part of their own future happiness."

Her cousin described his bargain with the Spirits. "My dream was simple. I wanted to make my ranch a success. The Spirits have helped me. Now my herd never gets lost in the mountains and never freezes in winter. The coyotes and mountain lions leave our calves alone. My horses never go lame. My beef brings the highest prices at auction. When that's not enough or when I need extra, money finds its way into my pockets."

So that's how he'd been able to afford such a flashy truck.

Her Cuz continued in order to show how she would be helped. "From this time forward, there will be people in each O'odham community that will speak for you in district and village meetings. They will speak and support your election as Chairwoman this year. In the future, they and many others will support your election outside the reservation."

The Big Man of the Spirits explained, "There are some in the world outside our Home that we will also touch. There are many non-O'odham who have made a bargain such as this, not with us but with our Brothers. Their obligation will be extended to include supporting you for whatever office you choose in the white man's world. Our Brothers in the Medigan world have used our Power and drawn upon our support to serve their purposes, and now we will use them for our purposes. For yours."

Juanita's Dad began speaking, using his own life as an example. "I received my gifts from these Elders many years ago, long before I met your mother. Knowledge of language and culture beyond what had ever been recorded: these were their first gifts. When I became restless just using the knowledge and skill here in our home, these Spirits showed me the way to become a Big Man in the outside world. They impelled me to my first academic post. Later, their servants created a post for me that granted me tenure and influence over the entire University system. They put me in the leadership of intertribal organizations—not just here in the US, but in the world. Their power extends over many people: O'odham, native people of the world, white people. I am what I am today only because they supported and assisted me."

The Big Man, spokesman for the Elders, began to speak again. Quietly, he said, "Little One, you have seen our Power and received our gifts, but you have not offered enough in return."

Confused, Juanita said, "But... but you have me. I have promised that at the end of my time, I will return here to be with you."

"As good a beginning as anyone could make," replied the Big Man. "But you know it is not enough by itself. We require more."

"I will actively support the causes and the people you instruct me to," she added, almost with a question mark at the end of her sentence.

"Good," he said. "That's another part of our bargain. Go on."

When Juanita hesitated, her Dad spoke up. "Commitment of your own spirit is not enough," he said. "Giving the Spirits actions they demand is not enough." He looked at the earth in front of his feet for a while before he went on. "When I made my bargain with the Spirits," he said, "I promised them the soul of my most precious love. It was easy. I hadn't met your mother. I had no children. I didn't have so much as a dog that I loved. Later, as my life went on and grew more complicated, the bargain began to weigh heavily on my heart. Your mother was happy with her art. She was satisfied with the tradition and creative expression in baskets that she had learned from her own mother. She wanted nothing more than what she had gained through love and family. Your sisters followed in their mother's ways and found happiness. I did not want any of them to be forced into a bargain with these Spirits. Then, I saw your desire and ambition grow, and you began to show you were as hungry as I was to achieve great things. I knew you would be the one to willingly fulfill the last part of my bargain."

Juanita thought about it, and seemed visibly shaken. "I accept this. But I have no one to offer, Father. Like you, long ago, I have no spouse, no children. How can I promise what I don't have?"

Juanita and her Dad looked at each other a long moment, not so much with affection as with understanding.

The Big Man of the Spirits broke the silence. "What about him?" he said, speaking low and looking directly at me. My heart pounded. I thought I had been well concealed, hidden in the dark doorway to the cave, but his eyes locked onto mine and his stare held me in a grip like an iron fist. The power in his eyes made me so weak that I dropped to my knees.

Juanita, her Dad, and the other Elder Spirits turned to look at the spot where he was staring. To look at me.

"He is precious to you, Little One, as you are to him. I see it written on your hearts." Hunger made his voice a growl. "Promise him to us."

I was dragged, still on my knees, pulled down to their end of the cave by unseen hands, Spirit hands doing the bidding of the Big Man. I was deposited in front of the cold fire next to Juanita.

"Tell him," the Big Man said to Juanita. "Tell him what you will do for him if he joins us."

She took my hand in the two of hers, and spoke low. It was the voice she used when her desire was in control, when passion ruled her. I'd heard it before on moonlit nights and in the backseats of cars, and it made me do stupid, wonderful things. Now it was the voice that showed that her need was single minded, and it left no room for thought or reason. "Make the bargain. Come with me," she said so low and with so much desire that she almost moaned. "We'll be together always, along the path. It will be glorious. Open your mind. I will be Chairwoman; I will make you Chief of the PD. I will be a Senator; I will make you top cop at Border Patrol. I will be President; I will make you FBI Director. Come with me! After our time in this world is over, we will be together for all time! Come with me!"

Her eyes burned a hole in my heart. Her words rubbed it raw. I ached for the comfort that I dreamed she could give me. For that moment, there were only the two of us in the cave, in the world.

"And who do I promise to the Spirits?" I asked myself. Then I asked it of her. "They won't take just me," I said. "And they've already got you. Who do I give them? An unborn child?"

Those words broke the spell.

Juanita looked away; she remembered her own betrayal in that question. Her Dad shrunk away from us. I saw that he felt more pain and shame than I had put into the words.

The Big Man of the Spirits spoke to me then, with anger too great to put into words, "Go! You no longer belong here. Never speak of this. Never return here."

I stumbled at a half-run back outside the cave. No hands helped me. I found the borrowed pony munching away at some grassy-looking weeds on the side of the hill. It's a good thing that he knew his way and took us home, because I wasn't seeing or thinking straight at that point. When Juanita and her Dad showed up down at the car at daybreak the next morning, no one said anything. No Where you been? No How's your Auntie? No nothing. They just got in and said, "Take us home."

We drove down the dirt road out of the ranch. No sign of Cuz or his kin. Maybe they all went to Church early.

We pulled out onto the Chiu Chiu road and headed north, toward Casa Grande. Dad was asleep already. We'd just passed the copper mine when Juanita, half asleep herself, said to me, "You know, they fulfilled their part of the bargain with me last night. I've got it all in my head. I'll be the new Chairwoman when I'm sworn in this June. There's still time to reconsider and come along with me," she said wistfully. Then, more confidently, she went on. "But I think they'll give me some more time to find someone to hold up my end of the deal even if you don't."

Maybe she had her eye on another fish in the sea, as they say. She herself would be a good catch. But my guess was there wasn't going to be a new precious love for her any time soon. Maybe the Spirits gave up on her making good on bringing them the soul that was the last part of her bargain. At any rate, that would explain what happened next.

We were driving around a blind curve on that Sunday morning road. A truck carrying sulfuric acid was heading south on the Chiu Chiu road toward the leach fields at the mine. It lost its brakes on the downgrade leading into the curve just as our two vehicles entered it from opposite directions. Acid is about one of the heaviest loads on any road, and the ol' boy driving that rig did a hero's job to keep his load on the road and upright. I'm a damn fine driver and Police Academy-trained in high-speed maneuvers. I managed okay to get us past the front end of that out-of-control semi, but we got clipped by the rear end of his trailer. It sent us through the guard rail at the edge of the road, and toward a drop-off.

I tried to not roll us over, by seeing how far I could make an unmarked Ford Crown Victoria Police Interceptor fly. I only succeeded halfway, and we wound up on our side in the middle of a rocky wash, with the car broken in half.

We scared the bejeezus out of some heifers, but there was no fire, and it wasn't raining concentrated sulfuric acid on us. I figure that the semi driver must've called in the accident, because my first coherent memory was when the EMTs rolled me up the wash to where the ambulance was parked. They told me I was lucky I'd made it. Seat belts and air bags are every driver's best friends, they said. My passengers, they told me, hadn't bothered with their seat belts.

"Some folks think they won't ever die," they said.

When the back doors popped open, well, the trauma from the crash had done them in. They were both well enough known that I didn't have to ID their bodies. I don't know if I had the gumption to do it at that point, anyway. I was numb and going on instinct and PD training. I don't trust my recollection of what happened in the time between the crash and the arrival of the emergency vehicles. You probably shouldn't either.

Before the EMTs arrived, I climbed out of the broken Ford and sat down on a big old rock in the middle of the wash. While I was sitting there—half conscious and wiping the blood from the one eye I could see out of—the Spirits came for them. They rode slowly, silently up the wash. The Big Man was on horseback and riding out front. There were Spirit Riders in a line after him that went back a ways, though their forms were hazy and indistinct.

Juanita and her Dad were just standing there in the wash, waiting, it seemed like. They didn't seem hurt or even dirty from the crash. They were just standing there waiting to get collected, like little kids at a school bus stop. I'll say this for them: there was no complaining; no whining about what should've been or what might've been.

Two Spirit Riders came forward and picked them up to ride double. The horses didn't complain—I suppose even two riders didn't weigh anything, being spirits and all. Then they all turned and started to ride off in the direction of the cave. But they just faded into nothing even before they made it around the bend. One Spirit Rider held back. He turned to me. He was skinny and looked like he was made out of old, cracked leather. I think he looked a bit like the old foreman. Maybe it was his great granddaddy or some relation. Maybe he was just a Wakial kurli, an old O'odham cowboy, with a message for us.

"Remember," was all he said as he faded. "Remember."

And so I do.

S IS FOR SUCCUBUS

by
Angelia Sparrow

IT WAS A slow Thursday evening. A light rain fell, turning the smog into mud on everyone's windshields and making the sidewalks steam. I had settled in with my good friend Captain Morgan for a nice, long weekend binge. Maybe I could forget some of the things giving me nightmares. Here in Memphis, being a private investigator and sometime skip tracer is one of the messiest jobs around. The only worse one is beat cop. The Preternatural and Magical Squadron isn't called The Bitch Patrol out of deep, abiding affection. Magic isn't good for humans. It makes us mean or crazy, or both.

I had emptied my pockets onto the desk: a crucifix (which was mostly useless except on brand-new vamps), Star of David (ditto, and it only worked on Jewish ones), garlic, wolfsbane, rose petals (all smelly), cold iron and salt (very effective), a .44 with silver bullets, .22 with regular ones (pretty useless), holy water (even less useful), and a couple ash stakes. One of these days, I was going to upgrade and start carrying a Desert Eagle. Sure, it only holds seven, but it has enough stopping power for things that the .44 doesn't even slow down.

I hate this town. If it isn't winter ice storms, it's summer heat and humidity. Being a normal who knows about the Nightside of Memphis only makes it worse. The Nightfolk know I know. The benign ones hire me. The nasty ones, well, let's just say I don't carry all that stuff 'cause I like the bumps it makes.

Me, I'm a No-Talent. That's someone with just enough of the mana to know about the Nightside, and maybe use some charms. But I didn't have enough to train, just enough to drive me straight into a bottle. No-

Talents have a life-expectancy of about thirty-five. I was pushing forty. Let's hear it for beating the odds.

She walked in the door as I poured myself a second drink. I couldn't tell much about her looks, what with that black cloak all bunched around her. Most dames don't go that big, though. I'm not exactly short, but even I don't fill the doorway like she did. She kept the hood up, and I only saw the lower portion of her face.

"Investigator Admire?" she asked.

"D.J. Admire, at your service, lady." My name is Dixie Jolene. I hate it almost as bad as I hate this town.

"Miss Admire, I need your help."

"Most people who come in here do," I told her and took a drink.

"My sister, Asanath, is missing. I last saw her going into a bar. We're from out of town, and she doesn't know where's safe and where's dangerous. She can take care of herself, but she hasn't checked back in four days. I'm worried."

"I don't usually take missing persons cases," I began. It was a lie, of course. I'd done missing persons almost exclusively for the last six months. I didn't want another one. The last three were all in various phases of dead when I found them. Dead comes in all shapes and flavors on the Nightside, and mindlessly loading trucks while bits rot off ain't the worst.

This gal bothered me and I couldn't think why. "I can make it worth your while, Miss Admire." Then again, the lady could be very persuasive. Especially when she sat that fat bankroll on my desk. "Five hundred dollars. Consider it a retainer."

"Fill out this form," I told her. I passed over the standard contract. "I get seventy-five dollars a day plus expenses for missing persons. Your bankroll will do for five days. I'll need all the information I can get on your sister, where she was last seen and that other stuff."

"Oh, you needn't worry, Miss Admire. My sister looks just like me." The lady unhooked her cloak and let it fall to the ground. She unfurled a huge set of bat wings. I'm no aerodynamicist, but I know there was more lift area on those than she really needed. The hood had been covering a set of horns and she grinned, showing a pearly pair of fangs. A slim tail found its way up on the desk and took over the pen as she stretched her slim, taloned fingers.

"No more sooky cases!" I snarled, slamming the glass into the desk. The last time I'd worked for a succubus, she'd tried setting me up with her brother as payment. So not interested in that. These demons never pay if they can welsh.

"Really, Miss Admire? Imarishka told me you were the best. I suppose I can always try R&G Detective Services, but I would prefer to deal with a woman." She laid down the pen and picked up the bankroll. "I'm staying at the Peabody. Contact me if you change your mind."

I watched as she left, and poured myself more Captain Morgan. I'd take her case, but not just yet. Sookies were always more trouble than they were worth. Sis probably just went to find herself some entertainment.

It started to rain harder. I hoped the infernal bitch got soaked.

After a couple more brief chats with my good friend, Captain Morgan, I caught myself turning the sooky's card over in my fingers.

All right, I'd give her a summons. I needed the dough. My landlady, Frau Blucher—name changed to protect the psychopathic—was making ugly noises about the rent. My license came up for renewal next month and my weapons' permits the month after.

I double-checked my bankbook, half-hoping I'd missed carrying a one and had suddenly found an extra grand somewhere. Crap, my bank account sucked. Missing persons only paid my dailies, unless I brought the person home alive.

I had to revise my rates.

But it was too late tonight. I'd get going first thing tomorrow. Or maybe Saturday. I watched the rain fall and killed the bottle.

Saturday after lunch, I took the card and went to the mirror. Most of my clients just use my cell-phone, but mine doesn't work across dimensional barriers. Something about AT&T not being compatible with whatever Bill Gates had set up for the outer planes in terms of telecommunications. At least good silver still worked across all the planes.

I read the card twice and took a nice deep breath. Stumbling on a summoning spell would get me hauled out to the Hell-planes a lot quicker than my booze would send me there. I gave the chant and she appeared in the mirror, pausing to check herself out.

"I'll take the case," I said. No time for chitchat. "Seventy-five a day, plus expenses. The five day retainer I keep, regardless of how soon I find her."

She nodded. "Agreed. Do bring her back."

"I will." She vanished and I stifled a sigh. Looked like the Captain and I had to postpone our serious date. I took a quick kiss from his sweet glass lips, capped him off and headed out.

I didn't drive, not for in-town work. The trolley ran late, and the werewolf behind the wheel looked worn-out but mellow. He gave me a funny look. Humans don't take public transportation much, unless they're poor or work with the Nightfolk. I was both.

I checked the moon phase on my watch. It showed a three-quarter waning. No wonder the driver—Chet, I read from his license—looked neatly shaved and mellow. I didn't approve of the current rash of lycanthropes moving in. The old Irish queens down in Cooper-Young had been all right. They, like this one, had been working. The local pack had gone to hell when Old Man Camomescro had died and his grandson Dan had moved away. They'd been good men, civic minded, not like Zoltan, an asshole who couldn't keep the riff-raff out.

Three years ago, we had one 'thrope attack, and that one a transient. This year alone, we'd had five, and every damn one had been a local layabout. If Zoltan didn't get things in hand there was going to be some real trouble.

At the corner of Beale and Riverfront, I rose to get off. Six shapes skittered past me off the roof of the trolley, heading down to the riverboats. Chet scowled and thumped the roof to dislodge any more that might be up there.

"Lousy gremlins on my trolley. Bet the little brutes were chewing my wiring for a snack as they hitched down to the barges."

"Probably headed to Tunica," I said. "Not much for them with Libertyland bulldozed." I hesitated a second. "Are you part of Zoltan's pack?"

He sniffed at me, a little worried. "No. He's a cousin, but I haven't joined up. My cousin Dan says he's a jerk, but Memphis is a great city. The wife and I love it."

So he had a mate. That always helped. Dan had been a local college prof, and a nice guy. I handed Chet my card. "If you or your wife need anything, I work for the Nightfolk."

He smiled. "I thought you looked tough enough to handle this neighborhood. How much trouble can we find driving and teaching handicapped kids?"

I looked at him. Unsmiling. "You'd be surprised." I climbed down and walked away from the trolley stand. He clanged on through the afternoon. I walked down three blocks and over two, ducked into an ally and knocked on a painted-over basement window.

"Yo, Mag. It's D.J. I got sugar."

A tiny pink hand, the size of a Ken doll's, poked out of the window. "Sugar first, Admire. You still owe us from last time," Mag squeaked.

I dropped a single pixie stix into the outstretched hand. "More when you talk to me, Magnolia." He hated the use of his full name. "Plenty more. I need to hire the Spyders."

"Door's open, D.J." Mag sounded mellower now. Wasn't even giving me a hard time about calling him by name. Pixies sure did love their sugar.

I went down the ramp and crouched when I opened the door. I duck-walked under the four-foot high ceiling down into the hideout. If you were a foot tall, the room soared vast and spacious. I was just glad I wasn't claustrophobic.

I sat on the floor and the Spyders surrounded me, their doll-sized bodies supported by butterfly wings that most of them had dyed black. Some of the males dyed them brown and put a black fiddle-shaped mark on the lower wings. The females favored red hourglasses. I knew those marks meant they'd made a kill. It might be a mouse, or it might be a human. I was always polite and kept my word to the Spyders.

Mag fluttered over and stood on my knee so he could talk to me face to face. His dye job had started scaling off, showing his real swallow-tail colors. He yanked up the collar of his black leather jacket like a tiny hoodlum, a move that would have looked extremely silly if he weren't a dead ringer for a foot-tall James Dean.

"Word is, Admire, finding that last floater drove you into the bottle." He fanned his wings in my face. "Sure smells like it."

"I only had two. Now, we gonna talk addictions? Because you know, Sugar Anonymous meets down at First Congo every Saturday. Pixies are welcome." I tossed another pixie stick out into the gang and they tore it open. "I'm doing missing persons for a succubus. Her baby sis went walkabout and the sooky's oh so worried. Betcha Lilith or Asmodeus is on her ass about it."

"Sooky?" Mag shook his head. "D.J., you gotta stay away from demons. Who's gonna bring us the good dope if you get Taken Outside?"

"Speaking of..." A female in a black corset dress fluttered up, bright red hourglasses on her dyed wings.

"Hi, Jasmine," I smiled. I pulled a bottle of Coke, the real cane sugar, glass-bottled stuff, out of my coat and popped the crown cap. I poured it into the big, shallow goblet on the floor.

Pixies can't handle corn syrup. It makes them belch fire. Which is why they let me know if they're headed out for a gang way and I set 'em right up.

They clustered around. I laid out ten regular pixie stix in front of Mag. "That's your retainer, along with the Coke. The job pays a case of Coke a week, guaranteed one case minimum." I pulled out one of those giant, two-foot-long pixie stix. "And ten of these."

"D.J., for that kind of pay, we'll ice anyone you say."

"All I need is info. Keep your eyes and ears open, Mag. Here's what your sooky looks like." I let the mildly telepathic pixies take the image I projected for them. Mental projection for folks who were already telepathic, about two minutes of precognition, and being a weirdness magnet were the extent of my powers. I hated being a No-Talent. "I expect daily reports and instant notification if you find her. There is a bonus for finding her."

Jasmine giggled and fell off the rim of the goblet. Some pixies can't hold their soda. "The Spyders are on it for you."

"Thanks, Mag." I left as he fluttered over for his own drink. Mag was a sloppy drunk and he liked big girls. I didn't feel like fending off an amorous Ken doll. I breathed the Memphis stench with pleasure once I had crawled back up to the street. The sugar odor in the hideout made my sinuses feel like they were stuffed like cotton candy.

I walked, making a mental list of places a succubus on the town might enjoy. Strip clubs, either to feed on the free-floating lust or pick up some cash working. Not the brothels. The vampire cartel had those sewn up, and nobody crossed the King. It wasn't a matter of living to tell about it. It was more like what the old man would do to you once you were dead.

Elvis's crossing over to the Nightside in '77 created a huge shakeup in the Nightfolk. He never claimed to be anything but white trash with more money than God, and the old-style superiority-complex vampires were scandalized. But he surely kept the vamps in line. We hadn't had an exsanguination in twenty-seven years. I didn't have enough clout to see my own vampiric territory manager, let alone the King. So screw the bloodsuckers, they weren't in on this.

Bars, casinos, and dance clubs. I could skip the Pumping Station and Backstreet, at least. Those were purely incubi hunting grounds. But I couldn't rule out churches. Some demons like the irony of feeding on the faithful. I didn't know how they managed holy ground and all that, but I had a sneaking suspicion it was because there was no such thing as holy anything. It'd sure explain why none of the crosses seemed to work. I'd

catch early service at St. Mary's, late services at First
Congo, the Conregationalist — Nightfolk and gays
welcome church — and then the evening one at Six Flags
over Jesus, or rather Bellevue Baptist. I'd check Idle-
wilde Presbyterian and a couple others if this ran into
next weekend.

I headed down to the bus stop. Presidents Island, and
maybe a run over to the truck stops in West Memphis.
Lonely men came off the boats and the road looking for a
lay. But the little lady didn't know what I knew. As we
turned onto the Island, I rubbed the odor killer I bought
from the morgue under my nose.

Used to be, this place shut down at five o'clock on
Friday, like all honest businesses. Then, about twenty
years ago, some genius got the bright idea of importing
zombie labor from the coast. Just like that, the long-
shoremen were out of a job and all their payroll went into
the bosses' pockets. A longshoreman costs forty grand a
year, plus benefits. A zombie costs about a grand. They
may only last three months in our climate, and they're
slower than mud, but they're cheap and tireless and
OSHA doesn't mess with zombie ops.

Nowadays no one goes to Presidents Island. Not unless they have to. This was a had-to, and I just wished I'd
had the sense to do it by day. My odor killer didn't cut all
the stink, and the poor truckers who hadn't known about
the zombies loading them, well, they all sat in their cabs
looking a uniform shade of sickly green.

A few questions of the dock bosses made it clear I
was the first female to set foot on the Island in a long
time. I headed back to town pretty fast.

Beale gleamed in neon, just firing up for the night, so there was no time for a shower to get the zombie reek off of me. Swell. I looked like a tough and smelled like a vagrant. The carriages stood in their lines along the sidewalk. Most of the drivers were human, but I spotted another lycanthrope in the group. Some 'thropes were very good with animals, while others couldn't get within a block.

Cinderella's pumpkin coach, twinkling with little lights, clopped past, filled with two pretty high school girls and their dates. The fake unicorn in the traces was a nice touch. I got a closer look at the driver, and decided someone had a better job scruffing up a real unicorn to look fake.

The girl behind the reins looked about sixteen, but you can never tell with half-Sidhe. We don't get too many down here. The way the moon caught her hair and seemed to shimmer on her pointed features gave her away to those who knew. Most of the folks just saw a pretty girl in rubber elf-ears driving a fake unicorn and hauling a tacky carriage.

The 'thrope, whose cabriolet I was leaning on, grinned at me. "I hate her. She works steady all night because she's so pretty. Half the girls are in love with the fairy tale and the rest, boys and girls, fall in love with her." He waggled his shaggy eyebrows, looking adorably puppyish. Most 'thropes past puberty couldn't carry that look off, especially the wolves. His horses could smell both the pixie sugar and the zombies and couldn't decide whether to nose at me or shy away. "Need a ride, Ma'am?"

I handed him a card. "I need information. I pay well for useful intel. I'm a PI and I work for the Nightfolk. I've got a succubus gone missing that I need to find."

"Not many demons around tonight." He sniffed at me. "You stink of silver."

I opened my shirt and showed him the heavy silver chain I wore. "Keeps my throat intact."

"Wise lady. I'll keep you posted." He tipped his hat.

I strolled off into the muggy evening. The thick air didn't clear my head, it just made it feel like my hangover was starting early.

I ducked into the Hellzapoppin' All-Demon Revue, the only all-succubus strip-joint in town. The succubus in mid-air shed her last stocking and turned a lazy double somersault. The applause lights on the tables flashed.

I ignored them and hunted down Nymphonia, the manager. She took me to her office just before the blaring rendition of "You Give Love a Bad Name" could deafen me.

"What do you need, Admire?" she growled. Nymphonia hated cops, and I was one step below John Law.

"Any new girls looking for work this week?

"No. Why?"

"New succubus in town. She's dodging her sister who wants to take her home." I passed over a card. "Look, if you get one looking, give me a call. I'll make it worth your while."

She agreed and showed me out fast. I didn't expect much. Demons were notoriously unreliable and Nymphonia had a talon in half the pies on Beale. She probably didn't remember me five minutes after I left.

I walked along Beale, taking in live music floating out
of doors and ducking crowds of tourists and locals out
for an evening on the town. It was late and I wanted a
shower, so I caught the trolley home. Our local combat
mage unit roared past on their motorcycles, on their way
to find some sort of trouble, or stop it. The Bitch Patrol
handled the ordinary criminals. The Delta Bluesmen
handled the big bad stuff before it could get to the rest of
us. A fine example of the mana making people crazy.

I glanced at the newspaper on the doorstep and compared it to the one on my desk once inside. Mayor in
funeral home scandal. Nothing new there. It seemed half
the local political family lived in the family business,
which was a funeral home. Even the ordinary folk knew
that. The paper made it sound like typical chicanery. My
paper read, *Undead voting rights in question. Mayor alleged to
be identity-stealing ghoul.* Same story, different spins. Dead
folk had been voting in elections for over a hundred and
fifty years, but it got trickier when some of the dead folk
sat up and demanded the right to pull the lever themselves.

I took a long, hot shower with the lemon soap and
went to bed without a drink. If I was going to early
services, I needed my sleep.

Church was a bust. Just humans at the services. St.
Mary's bored me and I dozed off at First Congo. At least
I sat in the back and didn't snore.

After a quick burger from the joint on the corner, I
documented yesterday's contacts, then made notes of
how much the trolley and the bus and the sugar had cost
me. I scribbled down the rest of the places to check. As

always, I left one office window open for my pixie informants.

Turned out, I needed it today. It kills my A/C bill, but the info pays the rent. The little cutie stood there on my desk, all purple spiked hair and black denim that matched her wings. She wiped her little brown hand across her forehead. The humidity made me mop my own.

"I'm Kudzu." She stood with her feet apart, her fists balled up on her tiny hips as if daring me to make something of it.

"Nice to meet you." I rose and went to the kitchen. I keep a box of sugar cubes for just such an occasion. I set it in front of her on a china plate from my old tea set.

"Mag sent me." She warmed up considerably after the first bite of the sugar. "We found your demon, yeah. Been eating pretty good. She's over at the Rescue Mission, yeah, sucking the souls outta drunks." She took another bite and looked up at me, looking a little drunk herself.

"Thanks, Kudzu. Enjoy the sugar and you can stay here until you're sober enough to fly. I have an extra bed." I gestured at the very soft Barbie bed I'd had forever. The sheets were clean, since it almost never got used.

"Thanks. You're okay for a Big."

I grabbed my coat and headed for the Mission.

Baby Sister had covered her wings with a cloak and her horns with a hat, but she couldn't hide her sexiness. The poor schlub lying limp in her arms had never stood a chance. She kissed him again.

"Freeze, Asanath!"

The sooky dropped her prey, already a shriveled husk that crumbled when she stepped on his arm as she walked toward me. "Hello, lovely thing. Are you lost?" she purred as she walked toward me. "It's not safe for pretty ladies to be out alone in this town, even on a Sunday afternoon."

I leveled a talisman at her. She just smiled, her fangs white in the sunlight.

"I know what you're thinking," I said. "You think you can reach me before I say the six word incantation. Now I've already said five of them, and being that this is a Chucalissa banishing totem, the most powerful talisman in the world and will send you straight back to the outer planes, you gotta ask yourself a question. Do I feel lucky?" I brandished the talisman again. "Well, do ya, bitch?"

All right, Dirty Harry I'm not. But I find the psychological edge that line gives me is invaluable. You'd be surprised how much you can accomplish in three seconds when your opponent is distracted by hysterical laughter.

Besides, I've learned a few things out here on the Nightside, and one of them is that demons don't watch movies. Act in them, certainly. Write them, of course. Finance them? Oh hell, yes. The whole points system is too fiendish to be the invention of humans. But they just don't watch them.

Asanath laughed and took another step. Oh well, I warned her. Under the Joint Planar Summoning, Banishing, and Transportation Treaty, that's all I have to do.

"Flxgeprt!" I yelled, wishing the nice little old talis-monger I bought my gear from would use sensible charms. But she was a traditionalist and liked her unpronounceable ones. She said it kept folks from setting off the talismans and charms accidentally.

Asanath vanished and the amulet felt heavier. A little anti-climactic maybe, but I never liked the kind that went in for big, showy spells. Fireworks aren't really neces-sary. Demons lie. I lie. It wasn't a banishment charm. It was a binding one. I tucked the amulet in my pocket, nice and safe, and headed home.

Well, crap. It was only a lousy two days plus expens-es. At least I got to keep the retainer. And there would be a nice bonus for delivering Baby Sister all in one piece.

I put Sis out on my desk and summoned my client. Kudzu had found the end of my breakfast coffee, with NutraSweet, and was lying on the Barbie bed giggling at something two inches from her nose. Fireballs from corn syrup, hallucinations from aspartame. My client came in, claimed her wayward sister, who was still in the amulet, and paid the bonus. In cash even.

Another successful case.

I had just unscrewed the cap on that nice, delayed date with my handsome, spicy Captain, when the next round of trouble walked through my door.

I hate this town.

UNDEATH OF A SALESMAN

by
H. Tucker Cobey

HERE'S A JOKE: A vampire hunter walks into a bar. The bartender asks, "What'll it be?" The vampire hunter immediately pulls out a crossbow and shoots him. When someone asks him why, he says, "Well, based on what he said there, I thought he might have been a vampire."

Jokes are funny for two reasons. First, the endings aren't what you'd expect. Normal society doesn't expect people to walk into bars and shoot bartenders with crossbows; if they did, people would probably tip better. Most importantly, though, jokes are funny because they contain an element of truth to them. And I guess the point I'm trying to get at here is, well, most vampire hunters aren't very bright. And are maybe a little too trigger happy.

I'm not most vampire hunters, though. I guess most people don't really think of it this way, but vampire-hunting—monster hunting in general, actually—is kind of a blue-collar gig. It's a physical job with lousy pay and worse hours. Most of us start off as apprentices to the older guys (of whom there are very few), or even just make it up as we go along. There's a kind of distrust of science and by extension education, too. Now, it makes a certain amount of sense. Science spends a lot of time telling us that the creatures we do battle against every day have never existed and, in fact, can't exist. Why would we put any trust in it?

This isn't too far off the mark culturally, either. Look at that seminal work in the field, *Dracula*. Harker aside for a moment, you've got two guys: Van Helsing, the brilliant intellectual who is the key to defeating Dracula, and Quincy Morris, the cowboyish, brawny type. In just about every adaptation, though, Quincy Morris goes away—and Van Helsing becomes Quincy Morris, or at least Quincy Morris with a much better knowledge of how to defeat vampires. People in general are not fond of intellectual heroes. They'd rather be saved by Quincy Morris. Vampire hunters, for that matter, would rather be Quincy Morris.

Well, I'm Van freaking Helsing.

The name's Joshua Slater. I'm a vampire hunter. Unlike most of us, however, I'm pretty legitimate. A lot of monster hunters just make their living by looting whatever they kill, maybe selling a werewolf tooth to a collector or dipping into a staked vamp's bank account. But me, I'm a private investigator. Which means that, yes, sometimes I spend my monster-hunting days seeing whether Mr. Jones really is cheating on his wife. The upside is, though, that I have a steady source of income when all the vampires decide to lay low and the werewolves aren't in town.

Don't get me wrong. There's a lot to be said for the "kill monsters and take their stuff" approach to life. I just look at it as kind of like a tip instead of my main source of income.

It was a Saturday afternoon when the call came through. I was in the office, which isn't what I'd prefer to be doing on a Saturday—but these days, I don't have a lot of choice in the matter. Business had been bad lately, and I was worrying about getting the rent paid. So sure, I'd spend a few extra hours in the office just in case a phone call came my way. The personal touch makes all the difference. And it paid off.

The instant I heard that familiar tone, I snatched the phone off the hook. Sometimes people get cold feet calling a PI. It's hard to ask for help. I wanted to make sure I got them before they had the chance. "Slater Investigations."

"Mister Slater," the voice on the other end of the line said, savoring every sound. I damn near fell out of my chair. Only one kind of voice sounds like that, and it's not the kind that belongs to someone on Team Human. "What a pleasure it is to actually speak to you. I've heard so much about you."

"I'm, uh… flattered. To whom am I speaking?" It's funny how even in moments of total shock, little habits like refusing to end a sentence with a preposition stick with you.

"Why, don't you know?" The voice was apparently amused by this. "This is Vincent Spyre."

Having just regained my balance in my chair, I damn near fell right out again. Vincent Spyre is the Duke of Los Angeles—in other words, he's the head vampire in the city. He's also the de facto most powerful vampire in California, which gives him a lot of clout on the national level. What I'm trying to say, here, is that my vampire-hunting butt had just been phoned up by the closest thing the vampires have to the Queen of England.

"Right. Hey. Uh… I don't want to sound rude, Your Grace, but why in the world are you calling me?"

"Why would anyone ever call a private investigator, Mister Slater?" Definitely amused. This was not good. "I want to engage your services."

I didn't even have a reply to that. I just sort of sat there with the phone up against my ear. Finally, I cleared my throat. "I'm sorry? You want to hire me to hunt a vampire?"

"Precisely." Suddenly Spyre's voice was deathly serious. "I'm sure you know, Mister Slater, that we have our own offices to take care of such matters. Unfortunately, they have failed us in this case, and the issue is a pressing one. In my estimation, you are rather uniquely qualified to assist us in this matter."

"I'm going to need a few more details than that before I take a case from a vampire," I said.

"Of course," Spyre said, his voice smooth. "I'll have an associate of mine meet with you in person to discuss the details."

I leaned back in my chair. "How am I going to put this? How can I be sure that this isn't a trap to kill me?"

"For the same reason I am certain you won't use this opportunity to send my associate to an eternal repose," Spyre replied. "The meeting will be in a public place — crowded, even. It's all arranged. All you have to do is show up."

I thought about it for a second. Pretty much all of my traditionalist instincts were against this move, but to be honest, I was curious. A case that the vampires couldn't handle themselves, and they came to me? It was oddly flattering. I looked around my office and began to notice little things. Walls in need of paint, dented furniture, that sort of thing. I sighed.

"Against my better judgment, I'll do it."

"Excellent. Look for my associate at eleven o'clock Saturday night. Don't worry. You'll know him." Suddenly Spyre's voice regained its amused quality.

I sighed again. "And where, exactly, will I be meeting this associate of yours?"

Spyre told me. I groaned.

"VAMPIRES AND THEIR freaking sense of humor." I took a sip of my incredibly overpriced cocktail as I looked around for whatever the tolerable number of times was, plus a couple. Not only did I hate this place, I didn't know a hunter that didn't. If you were the kind of person who got their kicks either by pretending to be a vampire or being "adventurous" enough to hang out with all the people who did, Club Nefarious was the right place for you. The decor was stereotypical red velvet with a touch of cathedral. The music... well, actually, the music wasn't that bad. I'm not that great of a dancer, but at least the beat got my pulse pounding.

Not that it really needed the help. Crowd or not, I still wasn't too keen on this whole meeting-the-vampires thing.

"Well, well, you actually came. I have to admit, Slater, I'm impressed."

I had been fairly certain that I was doing a good job watching the crowd, so of course the voice had come from directly behind me. I did what I considered to be a passable job of not jumping out of my skin then turned around to face the speaker.

"I couldn't pass up a chance to see why the high and mighty bloodsuckers of Los Angeles felt the need to come to little old me."

The vampire rolled his eyes. "Yes, yes, among the mortal servitors of the etcetera, you are a truly special snowflake. Now get over yourself, we've got business to talk about."

I frowned. This was not how vampires normally talked. "Who are you, exactly?"

"What, they didn't tell you? No, actually, I'm not even surprised." The vampire sighed. "The name's Deacon, and yes, I'm a vampire. I'm also the new kid on the block, relatively speaking, which is how I got stuck with the come-to-meet-the-hunter duty." I must have looked confused, because Deacon rolled his eyes again. "Look, you know how you thought this was a setup? Well, there's a betting pool going on whether or not you would stake me on sight. Which is nice, because maybe I can make an extra buck or two in Vegas with the winnings when we're done here."

"Right," I managed. "Well, far be it from me to keep you from Vegas for too long. What's the job?"

Deacon got a funny look on his face. "Mind if I sit down?" I frowned again, but nodded. Deacon sat at the bar next to me, but backwards, his face towards the crowd. For a second, he didn't speak. When he did, there was an odd sort of wistfulness in his voice.

"You know, I was a club kid back in the day. Used to go to a lot of places like this. We all thought we knew everything back then." I didn't say anything. If vampires have one thing in common, it's that they like to hear the sound of their own voices. The difference between me and most other hunters, though, is that I know how much I can learn by just letting them talk. "But tonight, I've had three people come up to me and tell me how I'm dressed all wrong for a vampire." I couldn't help but laugh. He smiled a bittersweet smile.

"Right? It's ridiculous. But that's the thing, Josh — can I call you Josh?" He didn't wait for a reply. "The world is passing me by. I'm stuck. I've only been a vampire for half a decade or so, and already I feel out of place, trapped in the past. I'm set in my ways. I struggle to keep up."

I nodded slowly. This helped to confirm something that I'd long suspected. More than a few of the kills to my name had come from a vampire that, no matter how smart they were, fell into patterns too easily predicted. "Sure, Deacon. But what does this have to do with me?"

"Everything," Deacon said, looking me straight in the eye. "Let me put it to you this way. You ever tried to teach someone who's substantially older than you how to use any sort of electronic device? Computer, phone, website, anything like that?"

"Sure," I said, shrugging. Deacon nodded.

"Now imagine trying to do that for someone who's really six hundred years old."

I blinked. I'd never thought of it that way. "You're saying vampires can't keep up with technology?"

"Not just technology. Everything. Slater, there are vampires out there who still don't understand how a car works. Oh, they're the rare exceptions, but they've had a hundred years to figure that one out. That's part of the reason that, every so often, they embrace someone like me." Deacon smiled humorlessly. "I might not be as... aristocratic as they prefer, but I might also be the only vampire in Los Angeles that's not computer-illiterate. They need you for much the same reason."

Deacon reached down toward the floor and brought up a messenger bag. He fished around in it for a moment then pulled out a folder with several sheets of paper. On top was a drawing of a dignified-looking older man. "Recognize him?" I shook my head. "That's Avery Brixton. He was one of the few vampires that could keep up. Having solid investments is about a million times more important when you're going to live forever, and Brixton took care of a lot of money for the LA vampire community."

"'Took care of?'" I cocked an eyebrow. "Something happened to him?"

Deacon's smile once again lacked humor. "Better believe it. See, it turns out that good old Avery was running a massive con on the LA dead. He was getting rich off of most of us not understanding how the stock market worked. As long as the money kept coming, he could spin any explanation he wanted."

"Ah." Things were beginning to come together. "And from your use of the past tense, I take it that someone wasn't too happy about that?"

This got a smirk out of Deacon. "Correct. And we want you to find out who."

I shook my head. "I'm still not seeing it. Don't you all have some kind of enforcer-detective?"

"We do, Slater, but this is what I was talking about when I mentioned needing someone like you." The vampire steepled his hands. "The Executor—the person you mentioned—first gained the job almost a century ago, and was a bounty hunter in the old West during her human years. No one in our community knows how to tackle this case, Slater. We need a detective of the modern age, and we need one that's used to tracking vampires. We need a hunter with investigative training. In short, we need you."

"Huh." I rubbed my chin. I had to admit it made sense. While pretty much any private investigator—or the police, for that matter—would have been suitable to solve the crime, there weren't many that knew about the existence of vampires. In fact, I'd made a pretty penny by offering to take as referrals any of the "crazy" clients who came to the unaware PIs talking about vampires. On the flip side, most of the hunters I knew weren't exactly famous for their intellectual heavy lifting. At least as far as LA went, it pretty much had to be me.

"All right," I said, looking at Deacon. "Let's say I sign on. Let's say your team gives me the promise of safety I'd require to do the job. One question: What's my guarantee that you don't come after me once the case is over? I'm going to have to open up to you all about a lot of my methods and resources in order for this to work."

"That would be part of the payment," Deacon said. "The Duchy of Los Angeles is willing to offer you a truce, essentially. Our word that, until such time as you attempted to slay a vampire without the Duchy's approval, you would be unmolested by the vampires who swore it allegiance as well as any guests of the Duchy."

"And how far can I trust your word?" I said.

Deacon looked back at me with a barely-restrained anger. "You can trust it to the end of the world, hunter," he said in a very dangerous tone. "We must keep ourselves hidden, and we do not trust easily. When we give our word, we keep it. The reason that Brixton's death requires investigation is that it was unsanctioned. He was a liar and a cheat. No one mourns his passing, and all believe that he got what he deserved."

"I see. I'm sorry if I offended." That was something I'd never expected to say to a vampire.

Deacon nodded, calming a little. "Apology accepted. Everything you need to know for the job is in the file. One more condition, though."

"Yeah? What's that?"

"I'll be accompanying you as the Duchy's eyes and ears on the case." He smiled again. This time, it was a little sardonic. "The boss wants to make sure that you don't see anything you're not supposed to—or at least, not too much of it."

I sighed. "You had better pay me extremely well for this."

"Oh, don't worry about that. Trust me, we've the incentive to give you so much that you want to retire." Deacon's eyes gleamed. I suspected that he had just made a joke. "Now come on. We don't want to keep the Executor waiting."

"Waiting where?"

"Where else? The scene of the crime."

MY SENSES CLICKED on the minute I turned the handle on the door. No signs of forced entry. The killer probably knew the victim. Vampires didn't keep their hold on eternal life by being the type of people to leave their doors casually unlocked. I stepped through, Deacon followed, and I got my first look into the mind of the vampire whose death I was trying to unravel.

The Santa Monica apartment was less spacious than I'd been expecting, but it was still palatial compared to the dump I live in. It was also one of those ultramodern places with lots of glass and sharp edges. This was pretty unusual. Like Deacon had described earlier, most cultural trends tend to pass vampires by—including interior design. Avery Brixton was clearly not the typical vampire, though. If he had been, they'd have never brought me in on the case.

A set of stairs—transparent panels, plastic or glass or something—led down towards the living room area. Two figures were there. One of them was on the ground and covered in blood; this, I assumed, was the victim. The other, standing above him, turned to face us as we came in.

I've been doing this vampire hunting thing for a while, so understand what I mean when I say this woman sent a shiver down my spine. The really powerful vamps have a sort of aura emanating from them, a kind of presence that can just about knock you off your feet. This one had it, and in spades. Black hair cropped to the length of her chin framed a face that would have put her in her mid-to-late thirties had she still been human.

Boots, jeans, and a long leather duster—all black—held a body that was whipcord-thin and tightly muscled. But from the moment she first turned to me, her eyes grabbed my attention and never gave it back.

Those eyes. Tinted glasses couldn't hide blue-grey eyes like a hurricane, like a flash flood, like a tornado in a blizzard. Looking into her eyes was like staring down a stampede of wild horses: You knew that what you were looking at wasn't a being so much as a force of nature. This was the Duke's right-hand woman. This was one of the most powerful vampires on the West Coast.

This was the Executor. And she was staring right at me.

Fortunately for me, Deacon broke the ice. "Madame Executor. I've brought the hunter." I blinked, and nodded. The Executor didn't say anything. Clearly a little more was expected. Against my better judgment, I cleared my throat and stepped forward.

"Joshua Slater, ma'am, of Slater Investigations. I'm, uh, glad to be of assistance."

"Sure." The Executor sounded a little skeptical. To be fair, so was I. She held her gaze a little longer, then snapped back to looking at the victim. "Lizbeth Davison, LA Executor. The hell took you so long?"

I glanced back at Deacon, who shrugged. He may have had a small smirk. This moved me from slightly intimidated to slightly annoyed. I turned to the Executor and jabbed a thumb back to the other vampire. "I let him do the driving."

That actually got a grunt and a small smile out of her. Out of the corner of my eye, I saw Deacon's smirk slip into an irritated scowl. Not that I minded scoring some points at his expense. Now we were both annoyed. Fair's fair. I started down the stairs. "So, what've we got here?"

"Victim's Avery Brixton. Turned at forty-five, back in nineteen eighty-three." Davison's voice was clipped and professional. "Kind of an interesting case here. Staked and severed, of course." Staking a vampire through the heart paralyzes them; doing that and cutting their head off is the only way to kill them permanently. Generally, you stake them first and then cut their head off—it's easier that way. "The knife's still here. They got a little extra use out of it, too." She moved aside, and I quickly saw what she meant: Whoever had killed Avery had stabbed out his eyes, too. It was pretty gruesome, but I was used to that in this line of work. I shot her a look.

"Personal, then. No one takes out someone's eyes like that unless it's a matter of vengeance."

Davison cocked an eyebrow. "Someone's been studying their forensic psychology."

I shrugged. "Vampires don't leave prints. I've gotta take the edges I can get."

"Puts you ahead of most hunters, I have to say." She smirked. I frowned.

"And you're ahead of most vampires. Don't think I know too many who keep current on forensics."

"I was law enforcement back in my day. Course, that was over a hundred years ago, but I like to keep up." Davison looked back down at the body. "Dead or not, there's always forensics. Course, I liked it better back in my mortal days. Back then, I could just shoot criminals."

I looked nervously at Deacon. His face was serious. Clearly, she wasn't joking. "Right," I managed. "So what've we got for forensics?"

"Well, we've got the stake and sever and the eyes, for starters," Davison said, all business again. "Here's the interesting bit: There're no defensive wounds."

My eyebrows shot up. "So this wasn't just an attack. The killer got close and staked him in one blow?"

Davison nodded. "One blow. Means this is a vampire."

I reluctantly nodded. One of the reasons hunters tended to have such short lifespans was that, generally speaking, vampires of any age were faster and stronger than us. It took real combat training to stand a chance against one, and even with that, staking one in one shot was just beyond mortal capability. "So. A vampire with a personal vendetta. Who could that be?"

"And now we come to the reason that you're here." Davison pointed to a piece of paper lying next to the body that I'd not noticed before. Frowning, I picked it up.

"To whoever finds this: Avery Brixton cheated us and stole from us. He has repaid the sum in full with his blood," I read out loud. Davison nodded.

"This is what led us to look into his finances. Deacon can tell you more about that." She looked at Deacon expectantly; he grimaced, but explained.

"He had some files on his computer. Spreadsheets, that sort of thing. I'm no financial genius, but even I could see that something was up. There definitely wasn't enough money coming in to justify what he was promising to my brethren."

I rubbed my chin. "I see. Can I take a look?" Deacon looked at Davison, who nodded. He motioned me towards the desk. I took a seat in front of one of those ultra-thin laptops that seem to be so popular. Touching it gingerly so as not to break it in half—something I always worry about with these things—I began to look through the files available.

In a few seconds, I was nodding. "He pulled a fast one on you, all right. Looks like a basic Ponzi scheme."

Davison made a noise of frustration. I turned to look at her. "A Ponzi scheme's actually a pretty old con. Basically, you tell people that you know this great stock or whatever, and they can get in on the action if they let you handle the money. So you get money from them, and use their own money to pay them a percentage every so often while assuring them that they're actually making money. When the original money starts to run out, you get more investors to put money in so you can keep paying everyone back 'interest' or 'dividends' or whatever you want to call it. Of course, the whole thing falls apart if you either stop getting new money in or someone wants to take theirs out."

Davison growled. "This whole thing is too complex for me. Times like this, I miss just shooting people."

I smiled humorlessly. "That's actually kind of the point. People like Brixton trust that the marks don't look too closely at the numbers. Out in the human world, they've got experts in this kind of thing, but…"

"In the vampire world, we need to have turned someone to even have a hope of understanding this. And there isn't a lot of glamour in turning numbers people." Deacon looked at the Executor. "Right?"

"Precisely," she said, looking at Deacon. "Your own turning was a bit of an exception to our normal pattern."

Interesting, I thought. I filed it away for further consideration then coughed. "Well, anyway, this guy was a crook. He got what was coming to him, far as I'm concerned."

"If what you say is true, he certainly did," Davison said, smiling a humorless smile of her own. "The punishment for lying and cheating is grave indeed. But," she said, her face growing dark, "this killing was not done by me, and is therefore a crime in and of itself. We have laws. They were not followed. And for that, someone must suffer the consequences."

Seeing her like that, I got another chill down my spine. "Uh, sure. Do you have a list of his business partners?"

"There's some kind of list on the computer," Deacon interjected. "A file format I don't recognize."

I frowned and turned back to the monitor. "Where?"

"There," Deacon said, pointing to the screen.

I sighed. "It's just a contact file. My phone can read them."

"Then tell your phone to do the work," Davison growled, clearly impatient with all this technological sorcery. I hastily emailed the file to myself, opened it with my phone, and showed it to her.

"Got it."

"Good. I would advise starting with those contacts," Davison said.

"Not a bad idea," I replied, turning to leave. Then I stopped and turned back. "One more thing. Who found the body?"

"The body was found by Brixton's youngest childe. Absalom, I believe he calls himself." She waved her hand dismissively. "I've spoken to him already, but you're welcome to do so again if you like."

"I'll do that," I said, and headed for the door. With my hand on the knob, Davison's voice made me turn.

"Hunter," she said, her voice cold, her eyes piercing. "Remember one thing. The Duchy seeks justice in this matter. You are a killer of our kind. If you are attacked, we give you leave to defend yourself. But if not, you are to leave the murderer to me. Is this understood?"

I nodded hastily. I didn't mind leaving the killing to the heavyweights. But even so, I would have agreed to anything when faced with those fearsome eyes.

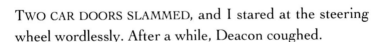

TWO CAR DOORS SLAMMED, and I stared at the steering wheel wordlessly. After a while, Deacon coughed.

"I might not be getting older anymore, Josh, but I'm certainly not getting any younger. Can we, perhaps, be on our way?"

"Yeah, just as soon as I figure out where we want to start." I pulled out my phone and tapped it against my other palm. "We've got the list of associates, and we've got the guy Brixton turned. Normally I'd start with the childe, but Davison apparently did that work already. Of course, the question then becomes whether or not I trust her to have been as thorough as I'd like. Also, don't call me Josh."

Deacon shrugged. "Davison is known among our kind as a woman of decisive action. That's good for an Executor who catches criminals on the run, but she's not always one for comprehensive investigations. The childe is the obvious candidate for murderer, but I assume that if she cleared him, she had good reason. It's up to you. Why can't I call you Josh?"

"It's weird, okay? I'm not used to having vampires call me Josh." I sighed. "I think we'll start with the childe. You're right that he's the obvious suspect—and if you want something done right, it's best to do it yourself."

Deacon shrugged again. "Whatever you say, Josh."

I started the car. "I hate you so much, Deacon."

THE MAN WHO opened the door of the Redondo Beach house was youngish. He couldn't have been more than twenty-five when he had been embraced. Good-looking, I guess. I don't really notice those kinds of things. What I noticed was the dismayed expression on his face. "Deacon. This is about Brixton, isn't it?"

"That's right," Deacon said with a smile. "Want to let us in so we can talk about it?"

"Why don't you come back some other time?" Absalom said, trying to close the door. I shoved myself in the way.

"Absalom, we didn't just fight fifteen miles of traffic on the 405 so you could close a door in our faces," I said. "Now come on. Let us in."

Absalom grimaced and sighed, but opened the door wider.

"Thank you," I said as I stepped inside, only a little bit of exasperation in my voice. Deacon didn't say anything, just followed.

We came into a living room with a lovely view of the beach. I took a moment to admire the scenery while the vampires sat down. Still felt a little odd to be able to let my guard down even this much around them. Once everyone was settled, I turned my full attention to Absalom.

"So," the young vampire said, "you're here about Brixton. You gonna try and get me to confess again?" I had expected hostility or fear, but if anything the vampire sounded annoyed. Deacon and I exchanged a glance.

"Not exactly," I said. "We're looking into his death. I haven't compiled a list of suspects yet. I just want the basic facts. Figured we'd start with you."

Absalom rolled his eyes. "Came to the right place, then. Not like anyone else was close. You mind if I smoke?"

I blinked. Deacon tensed. Vampires and fire did not play nice. Then Absalom pulled out one of those fancy electronic cigarettes, and everyone relaxed a little bit. "Not that it really does anything for me anymore physically," Absalom said. "It just helps me relax and think." He blew some vapor out of his mouth. "So. You want to know about Brixton. I guess I knew him better than anyone. I was his partner in crime, so to speak." Absalom smiled a wan smile. Deacon raised an eyebrow.

"So you knew about the con?"

"Knew about it? Hell, I was his protégé. He turned me about three years ago to help rope in new clients. A rainmaker sort of gig, I guess you could call it. Anyway, Brixton always handled the money side. He said that maybe someday I could move up and help take over." Absalom shook his head slowly. "I'm not sure whether he really meant it, but yeah, we always had a strong relationship."

"Really?" I cocked an eyebrow. "Usually I hear stories about you all turning on your creators." Out of the corner of my eye, I saw Deacon give a small nod. Absalom shrugged.

"He was going to make me rich, remember. I had every reason in the world to want him around." He took a drag from his e-cig and blew the vapor out, shaking his head slowly. "I guess the con might have been catching up to him, though."

I was about to ask a question when a harsh buzzing issued from Deacon's pocket. Deacon frowned, fished out his phone, looked at it, and then looked at us. "Sorry, I have to take this," he said, his face blank.

I frowned—what in the world could possibly be more important than a murder investigation?—but nodded. Deacon stood, gave Absalom a quick but tight smile then stepped outside. I turned my attention back to Absalom. "Why do you say that? Was something going wrong with the con?"

"Not in itself—just a conversation I had with him not long before he was destroyed," Absalom said, leaning back in his chair slightly. "You're fairly well-educated for a hunter. You're aware that vampires change their identity every few decades or so?"

"Of course," I said. "You have to. People tend to get suspicious of humans that don't age for forty years."

"Exactly," Absalom said. He took another puff on his e-cig. "Brixton had done that not too long ago—I think about five years or so, nothing in the grand scheme of things—but he mentioned to me not long before the murder that he was thinking of doing it again soon. Two changes in five years? That's pretty unusual."

"I'd say so," I said, nodding. Absalom's story lined up with my experience. I'd never heard of a vampire swapping identities so rapidly, barring a truly public scandal or a hunter making them as a vampire and then living to tell the tale. "So you think someone knew about the scam and was coming after him? That he was getting worried?"

"What other explanation is there?" Absalom said, smiling humorlessly.

I nodded slowly. "All right," I said, standing. "You've given me some pretty good leads. You want me to keep you updated on the case?"

"Please," Absalom said, rising as well. "I had a certain amount of fondness for Brixton. I'd like to know who did him in."

"You'll be one of the first," I promised as I made my way to the door.

"YOU WANNA TELL ME what that was all about, Deacon?" I said as I stepped outside. Deacon looked annoyed.

"Not really, no. What did I miss?"

"Absalom thinks that someone was onto Brixton. One of the investors is my guess."

Deacon nodded. "That makes sense with what we know so far. Losing your retirement fund is a hell of a motive for murder when you're immortal."

"It's a hell of a motive for murder even if you're not," I said, pulling out my phone. "Let's see... first name on the list is Franck Middleton."

Deacon whistled. "Franck fell for this? I'm surprised. Guy usually has more sense than that."

"Seems like good sense is in short supply whenever this kind of money is involved, vampire or not," I said. "You like him for this?"

Deacon blew out a hissing breath. "Franck's scary. Definitely has killed some people. Do I like him for this? Maybe. It's a little messier than I think he'd usually go for, but if he got angry enough..."

"Some things never change," I said, shaking my head. "Let's start with him." A pause. "Seriously, Deacon, what was up with that phone call?"

For the first time, Deacon gave me a look that made me remember that, for all I was starting to like him, he was something I should be afraid of. "Joshua. Drop it."

And I did.

"GOT ME DRIVING all across Los Angeles," I growled as we pulled up in front of the address listed on my phone. Middleton lived in a comparatively smallish mansion in San Gabriel, which, when combined with the driving I'd done to the scene of the crime and Absalom's place, meant that I was barely going to make any money on this job unless the vamps expensed my gas.

That wasn't actually the case, of course. It just felt that way.

The vampire who opened the door after we knocked was tall, slim, and black-haired. He looked a little like the kind of actor Hollywood would hire to play one of those cultured-yet-evil villains. He looked at me with brown eyes that advertised a frightening level of intelligence, then at Deacon. He said nothing for a second, and then cocked an eyebrow. "Deacon? I assume there's a reason you're bringing me a mortal?"

"He's with us. Sort of. For now." Deacon made a gesture of impatience. "You heard that Brixton's dead?"

"Please don't insult me, Deacon. Of course I know that Brixton's dead." Middleton's voice was cool. I glanced nervously at Deacon, but he looked calm. I tried to follow his lead.

"Well, Davison brought Slater here onto the case. Temporary truce, that sort of thing. There's a technical side that she doesn't understand."

"I see." If anything, Middleton's voice got even colder. "And what does this have to do with me?"

Deacon glanced at me. Great, I thought. He wants me to break the bad news. I shot him a quick death glare then turned to Middleton. "It looks like he was running a con. Basically, he was robbing people like you."

"Was he really?" Now Middleton's voice was frigid. There was a pause. "Perhaps you'd better come in," he said, stepping to the side and making way for us.

The interior of Middleton's house looked a lot more like what I expected of a vampire's digs: opulent wealth on display with a sort of mid-19th century Old World flair to it. I took a seat on a couch that was probably worth more than my apartment and my car; Middleton sat across from me, while Deacon stood. "So," the vampire across from me said, "explain the nature of this... con."

I pulled out my phone and looked at it. "What I have here," I said, glancing up occasionally at Middleton as I scrolled, "is a contact file with an entry for you. The entry has notes. The notes indicate that you were one of the first to invest in this little fund of Brixton's. That's correct?"

"I suppose so," Middleton replied, voice still chilly. "I was part of what he called an elite group."

"And by that he meant, 'had a lot of money and didn't really follow the finances,'" I said, pointing at the phone. "It says here in the notes that you're part of Group A. Now, I took a look at Brixton's spreadsheets earlier. Group A was the first group to get paid every month, so you got the fewest excuses, but you were all also in the deepest. If I remember right, you put in something on the order of fifty million?"

"That's right," Middleton said.

I steeled myself. "The entire fund had maybe ten million dollars in it at the time Brixton died."

Middleton said nothing, but his eyes flicked over to Deacon. Deacon quietly nodded. Middleton was motionless. Then, faster than I could see, he grabbed a candlestick on the table next to him and threw it through the wall behind him. I blanched. Middleton snarled.

"If he wasn't dead, I'd kill him again!" Middleton raged, then spun on me. "Human! Where is my money!"

"It's gone," I said. "Brixton probably spent it long ago."

Middleton snarled again. I winced again. His gaze bored into my skull. "Human. You should leave here now. Before I do something unfortunate."

"Yeah... I'm getting that feeling." I glanced at Deacon, who gave a fractional nod. With the minimum of pleasantries, we made our way out of the house. As we closed the door, we heard another very loud and very expensive crash.

"You believe him?" I said, looking at Deacon as we walked to the car. Deacon nodded.

"There's no way he faked that. We're a manipulative sort, but we frown on outbursts of anger like that. It's considered a childeish thing to do." He shook his head. "From a vampire of Middleton's age... It's got to be genuine. And it's probably good that we left when we did."

"I got that feeling." I sighed. "Maybe we'll have more luck with the next guy."

"NOTHING!" I slammed my hand down on the bar. "Dozens of vamp investors, and not one of them even knew a con was going!"

Deacon and I were back at Club Nefarious. We'd taken seats at an unused bar in the upstairs portion of the club. The music was still audible, but we were insulated from it both by distance and by a number of bodies near us watching some kind of performance. Not that I was focusing on that right now. I sighed.

Deacon shook his head. "I don't understand it. Josh, I'd swear that every single one of them had no idea that they were losing their money. Middleton was the least convincing of the bunch, and I'd bet my eternal unlife that he was hearing about the con for the first time."

I sighed and rubbed at my temples. "That basically leaves the childe. But not only does he not have a motive, he had the most reason to try to keep Brixton alive."

Deacon grimaced. "So we're out of suspects. Pretty much a dead end."

"And no leads at all to work with." I kept rubbing. There was a pause then I looked at Deacon with a frown. "You know, I wonder about that."

"Hm?" he said, frowning. "The dead end?"

"No. Your eternal unlife. Davison said something about it at the crime scene, and that phone call..." I let my voice trail off. Generally when you do that, people want to fill in the blanks. Deacon wasn't going to play ball, though.

"Suffice it to say, Josh, that people get turned for all kinds of reasons." The vampire looked out over the club. "Sometimes, the last person you'd expect gets picked.

You turn a conniving businessman, you get Brixton. You turn a Wild West bounty hunter, you get Davison. Hell, you turn some young thing who loves music, you get her." He motioned to the DJ on the dance floor below us. I blinked.

"The DJ's a vampire?"

Deacon looked at me as if I were a moron. "Josh, she hasn't aged in twenty years. Of course she's a vampire." He took a sip of his drink. "Not everyone's as blind as you, though. She'll have to disappear soon. I wonder what they'll cook up for her."

I frowned again. "'They'?"

This time, Deacon frowned right back. "Yeah, didn't you know? New identities are practically a community project. We need them almost all the time, what with not aging and you hunters blowing our cover."

"I always figured that they were sort of an individual deal," I said. Something was niggling at the back of my head.

"Josh, I'm one of the most computer literate vampires in Los Angeles, and I still don't follow what you did with the contacts and the phone," Deacon said. "It's pretty much impossible for someone to create a new identity for themselves. Especially in a community as small as ours."

I kept my tone guarded. "You mean it would be hard to change your identity enough that other vampires couldn't find you?"

Deacon looked at me oddly. "Like I said, pretty much impossible. Why?" Then he frowned. "You have an idea."

"I have an idea," I said, getting up. "Come on. I'm gonna need some backup for this, and if my guess is right we're not gonna have a lot of time. I'll fill you in on the way."

ONCE AGAIN, Deacon and I stood outside a door. This time, though, I was loaded for bear... or for bat. I could tell that some of my arms made Deacon a little nervous. Good, I thought to myself. Let him remember that I know how to kill him too.

I raised a hand and knocked.

This time, it was a few minutes before Absalom opened the door. He looked harried, and it seemed to take him a second to process who was standing on his doorstep. "Slater, Deacon," he said, distracted. "This really isn't a good time —"

"It's the best time," I said brusquely. "I've got important news. Mind if we come in?"

"I don't think —" Absalom began, but then I pushed past him and was inside. The apartment was in disarray; clothes and various other items were scattered all around. Near the middle was a suitcase. I turned back to Absalom.

"Going somewhere?"

"As a matter of fact, yes. I thought a vacation would be nice after all this." Suddenly Absalom was playing defense. "Can I help you with something?"

"Sure," I said evenly. "You can listen. See, here's the thing: I've been talking to the vampires who got conned by Brixton, and I've been noticing that most of them seem pretty irate."

"Ah." Absalom relaxed a bit. "So you think one of them—"

"So irate," I said, interrupting him, "that I really don't think any of them knew about Brixton's con before I told them. Would you concur, Deacon?"

"Sounds about right to me," Deacon said quietly, his eyes on Absalom. The other vampire frowned, looking back and forth between us.

I took a step forward. "So here's what I thought. I thought that meant we didn't have a suspect. But then Deacon filled me in on a very crucial piece of information. You see, I'm a hunter, not a vampire. A lot of what we know, we know by conjecture. Research. Old books. And I never knew that it's really, really hard for a vampire to hide from other vampires with a new identity."

"Yeah?" Absalom said. "What does that have to do with anything?"

"Well, see, it made me wonder about a couple of things. Such as, why would a vampire old enough to be running this kind of deep con think that he could just make a new identity to run away from it?"

"I don't know," Absalom said, his tone growing defensive. "Maybe he wasn't thinking. Maybe one of the investors got to him."

"And that was the other thing," I said, stepping even closer. "After talking with all the investors? I'm fairly well convinced that none of them had anything to do with it. They all seemed pretty upset to hear that there was a con being run. So upset, I'd swear that they'd never heard it before. So I gotta ask myself: Why would an old-school vamp with a good head on his shoulders run from people who weren't mad at him using a scheme that wouldn't work?"

"He wouldn't," Deacon said softly.

"Damn right he wouldn't," I said, looking Absalom straight in the eye. "So I ask myself, who's young enough that they wouldn't know that? And then I really have to wonder, why is the most obvious suspect in the case lying to me?"

There was a moment of silence. Absalom looked at me; I looked back at him. Deacon moved right beside me, ready to stop any move that Absalom made. I was armed, sure, but I was glad he was there for backup. For a while, no one spoke.

Then Absalom's voice filled the empty space. "He never asked me if I wanted this."

I stared at him. He looked back at me, speaking quietly. "I'd just graduated from business school. I was celebrating at a bar. I met this man with these fascinating eyes. He said he was with an investment firm that was hiring, that he wanted to buy me a drink. To help me celebrate." He laughed once, harshly.

"I took that drink, felt a little funny. I went to sleep. Went to sleep and woke up dead. That's when I found out the grand master plan. I was gonna be his business partner, his successor. An immortal rip-off artist, just like him. He'd turned me when I was young and good-looking. Between that and all the money I'd make, he said, I'd be a success like no one had ever seen. The world was gonna be my oyster. He looked at me with those eyes of his and said that he was my father now, and I was gonna make him proud."

A pause, then Absalom looked down. In a quiet voice, he said, "I hated those eyes."

I glanced at Deacon. He showed me his phone; on it was a text already written out to Davison. I nodded. He sent it.

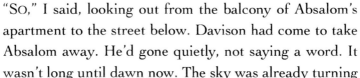

"SO," I said, looking out from the balcony of Absalom's apartment to the street below. Davison had come to take Absalom away. He'd gone quietly, not saying a word. It wasn't long until dawn now. The sky was already turning grey. Next to me, Deacon leaned his back against the railing.

"So," he said. "We call you in to solve some complex financial crime, and it's the oldest murder story in the world. Son kills father."

I smiled a tight smile. "I think 'brother kills brother' would be the oldest."

Deacon looked away. "Sure," he said. There was a silence.

"So what happens now?" Deacon asked quietly after a moment. "We go back to trying to kill each other?"

"I've been thinking about that," I said, looking back out to the city streets. "See, I don't know what the story is with you and the other vamps, but it's clear you're not in the most desirable position." Deacon nodded slowly. I steeled myself then looked at him. "And, well, we work well together."

"You're talking about making this more permanent," he said flatly. "A partnership." I nodded. "What will the other hunters say?"

"Deacon, half of them think I'm crazy anyway. And when word gets out that I've been working for vamps, I doubt they're going to start liking me more." Deacon nodded again. "So what do you say?" I said. "Worth a try?"

"Maybe." Deacon looked out at the greying sky. I joined him. "A vampire and a hunter, fighting crime. Maybe that's what our crazy little slice of reality needs."

"Maybe," I said, imitating his tone of a moment ago. He looked at me with a smile.

"It's a strong maybe," he said.

TAKING A BITE OUT OF CRIME

by
Mark Hague

MRS. TRENTON—better known to her TV viewers as Mandy Winger, co-anchor of the late night news on Channel 12—sat before me in a trendy lime green bolero jacket, a black pencil skirt, and a black satin blouse. Her dyed-blonde hair was styled in a pixie cut, and she'd already had too many face-lifts. Her long, sharp, red-lacquered nails drummed a steady tattoo on the armchair in which she sat. She wasn't happy.

"I want to know what's going on with Melvin," she said, slowly, lowly, and with a bittersweet undercurrent that belied the upbeat, downright chirpy voice Channel 12 viewers were familiar with. All twelve of them. I'm kidding. There might have been a few more than that, though not enough to warrant the large sunglasses she was wearing, inside, and her eager glancing around to see if she was being observed. I couldn't help but wonder whether she was angrier at her husband or at the fact that no one else in the office seemed to be paying any attention to her.

"He's always gone on nights of the full moon, regular, like clockwork. Each month. I want to know what he's up to. I want to know…" And here she lowered her voice and leaned toward me. I had to back away to avoid the wash of her undoubtedly expensive but too floral perfume. Sometimes having the sensing and hearing abilities of a wolf wasn't such a great asset, after all. "I want to know if Melvin is—is—well, a werewolf. If he's keeping that from me, well, I'll—I'll kill him!"

I could feel her pain, I really could. Her days as a news anchor were clearly numbered. She needed another avenue for publicity to keep her name and mug in the less than stellar night sky of minor luminaries. And if Melvin Trenton was a werewolf and she couldn't cash in on the cachet of being married to a supernatural, then what was the point of being married to him at all?

So saying, Mandy Winger Trenton pulled out a handkerchief to wipe her dry eyes—she wouldn't have been so gauche as to allow any moisture to test her waterproof eyeliner—and asked me to take her case.

Extraordinary Investigations was founded to help those with problems involving supernatural beings. I was a private eye even before that damned wolf bit me, so, being one of the two human faces of the organization, I did the face-to-face work with clients and handled the werewolf cases as well.

Finding out the secrets of errant spouses was the bread and butter of PIs worldwide, so there was no way I was going to turn down a lucrative case such as this, or turn down even a minor celebrity such as Mandy Trenton. I pulled out a standard contract, explained the terms and stipulations, and watched avidly as she signed and dated it.

Now, werewolves, as everyone knows, become more or less lupine on nights of the full moon. Since most people don't know any werewolves personally, they only know what Hollywood has shown them. And if Lon Chaney's version is all you've ever known, well, I pity your ignorance. No, there are as many different types of werewolves as there are, well, werewolves. Yes, some of us can become actual wolves, like in the Twilight movies—and I have to give thanks to that. Go, Team Jacob! But the truth of the matter is that werewolves turn into anything from Lon Chaney's hairy human to actual wolves. And our intelligence after transformation varies from no change at all to becoming, essentially, an animal with no human consciousness. The law doesn't make such distinctions, but requires all of us to be confined on nights of the full moon. And, yes, those of us who don't undergo any personality changes during our lunar periods resent having to incarcerate ourselves in home-made cages, or garages, or wherever for the duration of our 'lunacy.' As a PI, and despite changing completely into a wolf physically, mentally I'm still human, rational, so I have a special dispensation, though, like any aware criminal, on any of my special nights, I stay away from cops. It's hard to carry ID when you don't have any pockets to carry it in.

Of course, the rich are different than the rest of us. So, if Melvin Trenton did grow hairier and sprout sharp, pointy teeth on adjacent nights once a month, I was curious to see where he ended up. Rumor had it that those werewolves at the top of the heap in LA had a lair, or at least a private estate, where they went on our special nights that was stocked with prey—rabbits, goats, even cats and dogs 'rescued' from shelters—for their hunting pleasure. Those who didn't hunt were pampered, or so the gossip went, much like canines in one of those high-end doggie night spas. Their only containment was the boundary of the private estate, so they didn't have to be imprisoned in cages or garages or rooms inside their houses or apartments. Or so I'd heard.

Now, Melvin Trenton was a rich Hollywood agent and might very well go to such an establishment if he grew a tail on certain nights. I was curious to find out if the rumors were true. Of course I was aware there might be more sinister reasons for him to disappear on such nights—it was well-known that there were underground wolf fights on those nights, with the venue changing night to night, month to month. Despite the public outcry and police crackdowns, new ones would spring up constantly. Anything for a buck, I guess. It wasn't what I wanted to see or participate in, but to each his—or her—own. And Mr. Trenton might like to watch, and bet on, such blood sport.

There were also other, even less savory activities between werewolves and humans that could, and supposedly did, occur on nights of the full moon, sometimes in no-tell motel rooms, and sometimes in the clandestine bordello or two.

Werewolves transform not only on the actual night of the full moon, but also the nights that precede and follow it, making three nights in a row each month we become more or less lupine. And, fortunately, the first night was fast approaching, so I could, soon, observe my subject in flagrante delicto as it were (yeah, were).

During the days leading up to the first night, I trailed Trenton around town to learn his routine. I followed him to his office in Century City; to one of the nearby posh bars or restaurants, where he took his often mostly liquid lunches everyday, with clients and without; and afterward I'd follow him to either clubs, where he entertained his clients occasionally, or back home. Nothing really out of the ordinary, and, like a lot of surveillance, rather boring, mundane, but necessary. Without knowing what was routine, it would be nigh on impossible to know when he deviated from his regular schedule.

Then came the first night of the full moon. Trenton's day went swimmingly, apparently, and he had a three-martini lunch with one of his clients—a successful actor who'd starred in several blockbuster hits. A name you'd recognize. Soon after returning to his office from lunch, however, Trenton left and headed off towards Beverly Hills. Bingo. I followed as discreetly as I could, not so close that he would know he was being followed, but not so far back I'd lose him if he turned into one of the estates that dotted those hills to the west.

I almost did lose him when he abruptly turned into one of the estates in Bel Air. Fortunately, it wasn't in one of the communities behind gates where I'd have to flash my private eye badge and sweet talk a guard into letting me enter. I drove past, reconnoitering the terrain to determine the easiest entry. A stone wall surrounded the property, at least from the road and partially down each side of the parcel, but seemed to be easily enough scalable, at least to a person of my abilities. The estate itself appeared substantial.

I quickly found a place just down the road to park then went back to the wall of the estate. It was still late afternoon, and the moon wouldn't rise for a while yet, so I was baffled by Trenton's haste. It occurred to me that perhaps this visit was to a client and had nothing to do with his nocturnal disappearing act three nights a month. But since I didn't know for sure, I needed to get inside and find out.

I've alluded to an increased ability to smell and hear, but becoming a werewolf changes us in so many other ways, most of which aren't obvious to other humans. Yes, we become stronger, which, yes, sometimes becomes obvious with increased muscularity, but not always. Some of the runtiest, weakest-looking werewolves are also among the strongest, so one can't always judge us on that alone. We also become good climbers and can move faster, even on two legs. These are among the more common abilities we take on once infected with werewolfitis. Yes, that is a diagnosis now, but a syndrome which some of us, once infected, wouldn't want to be cured of. Certainly becoming a werewolf has helped me in my profession, such as now, faced with a wall I would have been daunted by in my previous existence as a normal human being.

I was up and over the wall quickly. My lupine ability to navigate through wooded areas also came in handy. The house was surrounded by woods, and I was able to skulk up to one of the first floor windows almost without detection. Oh, one of the guard dogs caught my scent and came growling up to me, but I gave him what I call my evil eye, let him see the hard hatred in my wolf's eyes, and he ran away pretty quickly. Domestic dogs, even guard dogs won't mess with a werewolf one on one. Not if they know what's good for them.

It had been a hot day. Someone had nicely cracked a window, and the conversation between Trenton and the man he was seeing was quite audible to me. At first it sounded like a bunch of business talk, and I tuned it out. Not my concern, though I continued to listen in case the conversation turned to something more interesting. And it did.

"Well, that's enough business," Trenton finally said. "I can take tonight's expenses off for tax purposes now." He laughed. "Good thing you're a client! Do you have my usual setup for the next three nights?"

"Come on, Mel." The other guy shrugged. I'd peeked and recognized one of the bigger stars of Hollywood. He'd have to be to afford an estate this size. "You know I do. And you'll like the ones this month, I guarantee it."

"The ones last month were pretty lame." Trenton sneered. "These better be better! I don't want to go elsewhere for my thrills, Dougie. And you don't want another agent. No one else can hardball the contracts for you like I can, right?"

"I know, Mel, I know. And I appreciate it. I do. That's why I've personally arranged the ones for this month. I had to really search for three wild ones. One girl I have for you is some low-level secretary, but a couple of the others are in porn. They're all supposed to be really wild during their nights. And they go almost full mode, just like you like 'em."

Reading between the lines, I grinned. So that was what this schmuck was up to. Mandy Winger Trenton was going to be so disappointed. No, her husband wasn't a werewolf. But he used werewolves to get his jollies. His sick fun, I assumed, included dallying with werewolf women on full moon nights, the wilder the better, with props for his panderers for finding those who would be able to change almost totally into wolves.

I had a camera with me and I could, if things went nicely, get a few snaps of him with a female werewolf to prove to Ms. Winger that I'd discovered her husband's sordid little secret. I knew she'd not find much cachet in a mere philandering spouse. Here in Hollywood, they were a dime a dozen. Heck, a dime for half a gross. Make that a full gross. No, they weren't uncommon, and Ms. Winger wouldn't necessarily want to spread this little bit of news unless she had an ironclad no-infidelity pre-nup or a good divorce attorney waiting in the wings. Those were a dime a gross here as well. Though I can't really complain about straying spouses. They pay my mortgage after all.

I spent the next hours watching the front door to see if Melvin Trenton left and trying to find a decent access to the mansion so that later I could slip inside and see what I needed to do to get pictures.

The minor movers and shakers, the ones who didn't have their own estates to roam around on, or who liked whatever amenities were provided here, began to arrive during the hour before dusk. It would not do to be behind the wheel when The Change came. When a sufficient number of people had arrived, I slipped into a tiny back room with a narrower bed than would be offered to an actual guest, so obviously a servant's bedroom. The window of the room, I'd discovered earlier, wasn't locked, and the room smelled as though no one had been in here for some time other than to clean. I stripped, hiding my clothes for retrieval later. Wearing only my camera, and making sure I could manipulate the doorknob with my paws, I waited for The Change. I was ready for it, had become inured to the pain as my skin erupted in fur and rippled, my bones transforming and internal organs shifting.

Minutes later with The Change complete, I resembled a small grey-and-white wolf. I put my paws up on the doorknob and turned it. Practice had made this easy, and I trotted out to where the others had gathered in the living room. I knew that those guests who were less rational had already been sequestered, probably in one of the adjoining buildings where they could be fed live chickens or goats in a nicely padded and appointed cage or room. The others, those who were mostly rational on these nights, were here, and I was amused that they still, more or less, acted as humans would in a social setting, talking in groups and lapping up wine from bowls on the floor, eating canapés and hors d'oeuvres from plates beside the wine bowls, while waiters roaming among them, bending down to place canapés on the plates and filling the bowls with more wine. And the werewolves were of both sexes, most of them male, but many women were here as well. Many had become mostly or fully lupine, while others still stood on two feet; although they, too, were covered in fur, and their faces and hands were more wolf-like, like Lon Chaney in *The Wolfman*. It was fun overhearing these men and women talking as though they were still dressed and at a cocktail party.

In the corner, in their own group, were several human men and a couple of women, among whom were Trenton and the actor host. As just another wolf among many, I was able to enter the room and mingle, getting closer and closer to the humans in the corner. Some of the wolves I passed looked askance at the small camera slung around my neck, but I figured as long as I remained confident and acted as though I belonged there, I wouldn't have any problems.

When I was close enough to the human group to overhear them, I stopped at a nearby cluster of mostly wolf-like werewolves who were chatting about the latest Industry numbers. I tuned their conversation out, while acting like I was following every word, and listened while the host explained the room assignments for the night.

"Trenton, you'll be in your usual room," the host said. Completely unhelpful. "Marjorie, you'll be in the room across the hall from Trenton's, in the east wing. He'll be in the last room and you'll be across the hall in the other. I think you'll be pleased this month. I've taken precautions so you won't get hurt this time. We found a better muzzle—he shouldn't be able to snap this one off as easily." Much better.

I trotted up to the second floor and made my way down the eastern wing to the last door. Placing my paws up on the doorknob, I opened the door and entered.

On the bed, a male wolf turned and stared at me, growling as best he could with a metal muzzle around his snout. Oops, wrong room. "Sorry," I growled in return. While I could still speak in werewolf form, my voice was pretty growly and my words weren't always as intelligible as I'd have liked. Still, I could usually make myself understood with effort.

I shut the door and crossed to the other side. Fortunately, there was no one in the corridor. Yet. On this bed was a female wolf. She wasn't muzzled but she was chained to the bed securely so she had no leeway to bite anyone who approached her from behind. Multiple silver chains tethered her to both sides of the headboard. For some reason, silver weakened us and proved to be painful if we were exposed to it for too long.

I glanced around the room for a hiding place. The room was poshly furnished, with a nice, big bed and high-quality chest of drawers, chairs, and a nicely carved, antique armoire. There was a closet but I didn't think the line of sight was ideal for a good picture. I held a paw to my mouth to indicate silence on her part, though I doubted that she could understand. She whimpered and I remembered the earlier conversation: that she was a werewolf who became more or less a wolf on our nights. I pawed open the armoire and was amused to see, on the top shelf, an elaborate setup with a camera aimed at the bed. With a soft red light that showed that the camera was filming. Fortunately, I hadn't gone close to the bed and hoped I'd remained out of the frame. Apparently the host wanted his own pictures of this encounter. To pique his own prurient interests or for blackmail? There was enough room inside the armoire for me, and I positioned my camera in such a way that when Melvin Trenton entered I'd be able to nose the door open a little wider and have a great shot of the bed and Melvin Trenton in all his glory. I closed the door as best I could and waited.

I didn't have long to wait. The outer door opened and Melvin Trenton came in, quickly undressed, and crossed the room to the bed. He patted the woman, making sure that his hand didn't get close enough to her mouth so that she could bite it. Restrained as she was, her head still had a very limited mobility.

This wasn't my first stakeout, but what followed disgusted me. I have no problems with sex between consenting adults. In my line of work, it's like watching terribly ho-hum porn. But this wasn't between consenting adults. What I had to watch that night was a rape. Whether the woman had agreed to it or not. What she was now was simply a scared wolf not in heat, which meant that she wasn't enjoying the penetration, so it was rape, even if the law deemed it, at most, animal cruelty.

What I wanted to do was jump out of the closet and stop him, call the police and have him taken away in cuffs, see how he liked being bound. But I was on assignment and I didn't know what the woman had agreed to. Perhaps, as a human being, she had known exactly what she would be subjected to, even if, at the moment, she didn't have her human reasoning to consent. The legal and moral ramifications were blurry. If she'd agreed to sex for money while a wolf, then this was simply an illegal transaction, and while I might agree that prostitution is demeaning for the paid participant, if the two—or more—are completely consenting, then no harm done. At the same time, this was morally wrong. The wolf no more wanted to be penetrated than any other victim of rape.

I snapped enough pictures to present to Mrs. Trenton. While in werewolf form, we're not considered 'human' by the law, but with even a mediocre attorney, Mandy Winger Trenton should be able to clean Melvin Trenton's clock, or at least wipe out his bank account.

Unless being married to the scumbag still gave her enough prestige in the circles she frequented.

Eventually, Trenton had spent his wad enough to fall asleep, as far away from the wolf's mouth as possible. It was a very big bed. Even the wolf, restrained as she was, laid down and slept as well. I crept out of the armoire and went over to the bed, trying, as best I could, to stay out of the frame of the camera, to see if there were any way I could unchain the wolf. But nosing around in the drawers in the table next to the bed didn't elicit any keys. I tried to think of other ways to free her, but the collar around her neck was securely fastened with a lock and without a key there was no way to liberate her. I thought I could perhaps take her out with me, but then, she probably wouldn't appreciate it if she hadn't yet been paid for this night's work when the sun rose and she was human again. Not to mention naked—I hadn't found any clothes that could have belonged to her in my hasty perusal of the room.

Melvin Trenton snored on, unaware of my presence, and I left, trotting down the silent hallway outside. While the hallway was silent, there were noises still loudly issuing from some of the rooms on either side—moans and sighs and more. I descended to the first level. There were guards, but I easily evaded them and returned to the room where I'd left my clothes. I waited there for the sun and The Change Back and the ability to use my hands again to get dressed and depart.

There were security guards outside as well, probably there to assist those who'd been outside all night and who were now recovering from The Change Back. Some would be disoriented and need help returning to the house and their clothes. I easily avoided them.

The front gates weren't open yet and I scaled the wall and returned to my car.

I called Mrs. Trenton as soon as I developed the photos and arranged to meet with her that afternoon in my office.

She was prompt, eager to find out if her Melvin was a werewolf. I told her she'd have to find some other way to augment her limited fame. She was disappointed by my findings and the pictures, but, interestingly, not outraged either by his infidelity or the rape. She paid for my services and left. I felt like I needed another shower. The case was closed. I'd write my report, then wait for the next case.

After she left, I did some paperwork, wrote up my report on the Trenton affair—though it was more like a one-to-three night tryst, if she was assigned to Trenton for all three nights. It wouldn't have surprised me if the participants swapped partners each of the three nights. Whatever. It wasn't really my concern what they did behind those giant, barred gates. Though I was still disturbed by the rape—I couldn't call it anything else, whatever the werewolves had agreed to while in human form. At the same time, if, as humans, they'd consented, then there was nothing I could do about it. The host had money and could probably bribe his way out of any charges of pandering or animal cruelty; if not, he could certainly hire a powerhouse attorney to provide legal distance from his crimes. He probably wouldn't even be brought up on any charges, not with his fame and money.

He might even be able to spin the situation as philanthropy—he was only providing a place for his werewolf friends to congregate during the full moon. It was unfortunate that some of them were used poorly by other guests. A shame, really. But he, of course, knew nothing about it. Yeah, right.

I wouldn't have thought any more about it if I hadn't happened to open up the newspaper four days later to see a photo of the woman I'd last seen tethered as a werewolf next to Trenton on a bed.

No, the photo wasn't of her as a wolf. It was her human face that would have stared out of the morgue photo if her eyes had been open. I, of course, couldn't be one hundred percent sure it was the same woman, but years of seeing werewolves in both human and wolf forms had made me pretty accurate in seeing the resemblance between the two. The accompanying story said that the body of this Jane Doe had been found out in the Valley the day before on an off-the-beaten-track hillside. It was pure chance that a man out hiking had been alerted to her body by his dog.

I called the police, asked to speak to whomever had the Jane Doe case, and told him what I knew. Detective Rogers asked me—which was more polite than him ordering me, but it amounted to the same thing—to come in to see him and bring my photos and then go visit the morgue to look at the body in the flesh, as it were.

I didn't have much cause to visit the morgue ever, and it was depressing, smelled like a hospital surgical suite, minus the smell of anesthesia. The bodies here didn't need anything to deaden the pain of being cut open. Oh, yeah, it smelled of death. I didn't like it.

While I wouldn't have bet my life that it was the same woman, my gut told me it was. Unfortunately, my gut feeling didn't count as evidence. And while the detective could go and question the host of the estate where the werewolves were entertained three nights a month, it was only my word against the actor's, and his word meant a lot more than mine.

I left the police headquarters and returned to my office where I scoured the usual sources to see whether any other bodies had been found following full moons in the last six months. It wasn't entirely unusual for there to be werewolf-related deaths during full moons—there would always be the rebel werewolf who thought he or she didn't need to be caged on our nights, and would be proven tragically wrong. Isolated reports over a month or two didn't show much of a pattern, but when I went back six months, one emerged.

I had actually begun my research thinking that, in the morning, Trenton had woken up and tried to have sex with the woman, either as a woman or as a wolf, that something had gone wrong, and the woman had died. But when I saw her body in the morgue I saw she had died from having her jugular cut, and that could hardly have been from an accident.

As I delved into the newspaper articles, though, I found other means used to kill the victims: some were stabbed, some shot, others poisoned. Murders in the greater Los Angeles basin were pretty routine, but there was a pattern of Jane and John Does—of course, more

Janes—the bodies dumped out in the valley or at the beach or in some out-of-the-way place. If I were cynical, I'd say far enough away from Bel Air not to be linked back to that estate or its well-known owner. I created a spreadsheet of forty-seven bodies, some since identified, that had been found in the greater LA area with a death date after full moons.

I called Detective Rogers and told him what I'd discovered. He wearily asked me to bring in my research. Of course, all I had was conjecture, since I was pretty sure the victims' bodies hadn't been tested for werewolfism—they weren't the attackers, after all.

Detective Rogers pointed this out to me, and while I acknowledged that such was the case, he did, rather reluctantly, admit that the most recent Jane Doe in question had been tested on my say-so. She'd been positive for werewolfism and identified as the werewolf I'd seen. I suggested, nicely of course, that as many of the John and Jane Does and others who had been identified after dying after full moons be tested as well, since the blood samples would still probably be on file, to see if they could have been werewolves and to see if they could be traced back to the estate.

I didn't have much to go on, and unless Detective Rogers agreed to divulge any other tidbits, which was highly unlikely, there wasn't much for me to investigate. Spencer, the head of our agency, grudgingly gave me leave to pursue this, seeing how much it bothered me. Of course I'd have to abandon my research if a paying job came in.

A week later came the first break in the case. The Jane Doe turned out to be Amanda Fuller, a secretary at Sparks and Hagel, a financial firm out on Wilshire. I called S & H and asked to speak to the head honcho, who turned out to be Marty Heinsman. I was actually surprised I'd gotten an appointment. Most higher-ups shunted PIs like me to either a lower vice-president or the head of HR. He was a nervous type, or perhaps just on edge that word had gotten out that he'd employed a werewolf, however unknowingly. His stockholders were not going to be happy.

Heinsman told me that he'd agreed to see me in order to see if I could somehow quell the media hullabaloo about the woman's supernatural disability, as he put it. I don't think he was an intentional bigot, but I promised him I'd try to help make the media attention disappear — as if I could wave a magic wand and it'd go away — but I would need the freedom to speak with anyone in the company in exchange. I took advantage of his 'generosity.' I was able to go back to Detective Rogers with a report and with my spreadsheet, and even as poker-faced as he was, he still managed to convey his surprise and interest in my research.

"Detective, while they 'officially' didn't know she was a werewolf, many of her co-workers and even her boss knew there was something 'different' about her. She worked there for three years and even her closest friends didn't know much about her private life."

"I interviewed many of her co-workers myself," Rogers informed me gruffly. "They only said she was a private person and did adequate work. How did you find out that they thought she might be were?"

"The police don't have my werewolf ability to tell a lie from the truth. Officially, no one knew she was a werewolf, but, unofficially, many of her co-workers had known something was 'odd' about her. Some even speculated that she might be supernatural, maybe a vampire or a witch. If the police department would stop discriminating against supernaturals in hiring officers, you'd have guys like me who can tell truth from lies, and there's no way to cheat like with a lie detector."

"Yeah, well, that's not going to happen anytime soon," he grumbled. "And whether you have such an ability or not, it wouldn't be admissible in court anyway."

I sighed. The same-old, same-old bigotry as usual — as with American Indians, Asians, Blacks, Mexican-Americans, gays, transgendered folk, and the disabled community before us, we supernaturals could still be discriminated against unfairly. But then, wasn't any discrimination inherently unfair?

"Detective, could I have shots of all the victims on my spreadsheet? I have resources you don't have —"

When he bristled, I did my best to calm him down. "Yeah, yeah, I know the police are good at their jobs, but I'm a werewolf, I know werewolves who know were-wolves, and I can show the shots around and maybe even get some of your John and Jane Does identified, if they were were. You can't do that. I can."

He wasn't happy about complying, but he brought out thirty-three morgue photos — considerably less than the forty-seven victims I had on my spreadsheet.

"As you suggested," and he glared at me as though my previous suggestion could be construed as having interfered in a police investigation, "we were able to test the tissue and blood samples on file for all the victims we think died after full moons and thirty-three came up positive for werewolfism. I see on your spreadsheet that you have names of people who are normal just like you and I—er—well, like me," he added lamely.

I sighed again. I was tired of the old us/them dichotomy. The Cro-Magnons had probably done it with the Neanderthals: "We're evolved, you're not!"

"Detective, we're now a recognized minority and we deserve to be treated like everyone else—"

"Yeah, yeah, yeah," the detective said, waving away my soapbox harangue. "Look, we're trying to solve these murders like we would for normal people, okay? So don't give me any grief." He tossed me the manila folder with the morgue shots. "I wouldn't be releasing these to you, but you've helped us put this case together. And, Heaven help me, I've got to trust you. Get back to me if you're able to identify any of 'em."

"Just a few more questions, please. Was there a recent deposit of money into Amanda Fuller's bank account? I'm thinking that she might have been paid for the sex? Or perhaps she was paid in drugs? I assume a tox screen was done on her body?"

"Of course there was. We're pretty thorough, you know." He glared at me. "That's our job."

"Which is why I'm asking, Detective. You may not like the fact that I'm were, but we're on the same side on this. You wash my hand, I wash yours, and if we solve these murders, you're going to look good, okay?"

"No deposits. No recent purchases out of the ordinary. Tox screen came back negative for anything out of the ordinary. And, yeah, I had the other victims tested as well. The same, or at least nothing recent. And the same thing with bank deposits for the ones who were identified. Nothing, nada, zilch. We didn't find anything to indicate they were paid for those nights in any currency we know of. But, of course, you werewolves — "

I thanked the detective before he went any further and I left his office.

There were, of course, other possibilities. Payment promised afterwards, or that the payment was being pampered for the three days and nights, or even that she hadn't actually agreed to be used for sex at all. Once at the estate, however, after she'd changed, someone could have collared her and put her in the room to be used by Trenton or whomever. This didn't account for her death the day after the third night of the full moon. She'd taken vacation from work, but surely if she'd been used against her will, she wouldn't have stayed at the estate each night — that is, if she'd known what had happened to her. Maybe she didn't. Many of us, those who changed most fully into animals, had a sort of amnesia with only vague memories of what had happened on those nights after The Change. Unanswered questions that would remain unanswered. I even considered paying Spencer, our agency's founder and the resident spook, to contact Amanda's ghost, if possible, but Spencer charged an arm and a leg, and I still needed mine.

I eliminated the non-were victims from my database. Of the remaining thirty-three, eleven had been identified. Those I traced. Most were low-level office workers. Some were prostitutes, and some were models or worked in the fast food industry or in porn. I interviewed their co-workers when I could find any, and most of those didn't know the victim had been were. There didn't seem to be any connection between them. They'd taken a vacation or a leave of absence for the three full moon days and then never returned. The only connection seemed to be that they needed money. One other tentative connection: these people had been loners, generally, and not much was known about their private lives.

I had been were long enough to have contacts that the police didn't. I knew a number of underground groups and clubs that catered to weres, so I made pictures of the John and Jane Does still on my list and started my rounds. It was a slog, going from group to group to group, but I was persistent and though I wasn't successful in fully identifying all of them, I was able eventually to amass quite a bit of data that might help identify these otherwise unknown people.

And though a case or two did intervene and make me lose some valuable time in my investigation, they weren't so time-consuming that I had to abandon my own case. Friends asked me why I cared, and I don't know if I could have honestly answered. But I did care. Maybe if I hadn't been there the night Amanda Fuller had been used and abused I could have read about her death in the paper and forgotten it three seconds later. But I'd been there, and I wanted justice for her and the others whom I hadn't seen. Even if they had knowingly signed up for sex with humans those nights, well, knowingly or not, their lives shouldn't have been ended because of it. They weren't expendable. Maybe to the bigots, maybe even to the police, but they weren't—not to me.

And so I continued. I knew, of course, that I couldn't identify every Jane or John Doe, but I kept showing their morgue photos to my contacts in werewolf circles. I was able to piece together a few more identities during the month before the next full moon, passing on any information I gleaned to Detective Rogers. I had positively identified twenty of the Jane and John Does. And I couldn't repress a smirk when he expressed shock that I was able to identify so many when the police hadn't.

Following another hunch, I had already started paying more attention to word on the street and responded to underground ads seeking werewolves during our nights. The next full moon was approaching, and I had to get back inside the estate.

It was past time to interview Melvin Trenton. He was the only one, besides the host, whom I knew had been at the party.

At first, of course, Trenton refused to even see me, especially when it was obvious I wasn't a high-paying potential client. It was still days away from the first night of the full moon and I had been insistent that we meet as soon as possible. Still, he tried to put me off until I hinted that I knew what he did on full moon nights, then he reluctantly agreed to meet me at a bar after work.

He was belligerent when he walked in an hour late for our meeting.

"Don't think I'm giving you any money, fella! So I play around sometimes. Who in LA doesn't? And don't think that you can blackmail me by threatening to tell my family or work. My wife already knows and I call the shots at work, so you're an idiot if you think I'm giving you a damned penny."

I didn't disabuse him that I didn't want any of his ill-gotten lucre. Instead, I thrust the photo of Amanda Fuller in his face after he sat down. Morgue photos aren't pretty and he blanched as any normal person would. It took the wind out of his sails as I knew it would.

"Who—who is she?" he asked.

"That's one of the werewolves you fucked last month. You tell me what you know about her, and what happened to her—why you killed her—and maybe the police won't get involved, got it?" He was a Hollywood agent and therefore a shark, but I was a werewolf and he didn't have a chance.

"I—I didn't kill anyone. I—I couldn't." Likely story; he was ruthless. "I—I don't know what happened to her. I left her in the morning, asleep. Uh—she worked in an office somewhere. I didn't know her. Really, I—"

I don't like babblers unless they were babbling something I didn't already know, but he did have info I wanted, so I cut him off. "Tell me about those nights at the movie star's house. How you heard about it, what you're promised, what you have to pay, everything. If I find you've left anything out, the police get everything on you, understand?"

Of course, he didn't know the police already had everything, and he told me everything he could. Rogers had agreed, reluctantly, to hold off until I'd interviewed Trenton myself. He'd have his turn in the morning after I'd divulged everything that Trenton spilled. And he spilled everything—how his client—the movie star—had initially offered him werewolves for sex and how much he paid for the privilege. I would have whistled at the cost, but I was trying to play bad-ass here, and wanted it to seem like I already knew everything he was telling me. "He told me that the women would be taken care of. I assumed that meant they'd be paid, or hypnotized or given drugs or something so they wouldn't remember what happened or who was with them. You gotta believe me."

I left Melvin Trenton downing whiskeys on the rocks, upset and scared. As he should have been. I still considered what he did rape, even if the law didn't. It was late when I called Rogers. He was off-duty. I didn't care. He did whistle at the amount Trenton paid each month for three nights of nonconsensual sex.

About the same time the next day that Detective Rogers was grilling Trenton, I was responding to an ad that purported to hire young and attractive werewolves to attend parties. Uh-huh.

Well, I wasn't so young anymore, and perhaps attractive was debatable as well, but I cleaned up well, arriving at the address I'd been given: a nice office out on Wilshire Boulevard, actually not that far from Sparks & Hagel. The woman interviewing me had specific questions, such as my availability during the full moon, my regular employment, name, address, all of that. I answered all the questions in a way that I thought they'd like, especially those that were more personal such as how much I changed during The Change and what happened to me when I did. I must have passed their initial screening for I was asked back to speak to a higher-up.

My 'cover' was that I worked at a firm, but had gambling debts and needed extra money, that I changed into a wolf completely on the full moon nights, and that I had little recollection of what happened on those nights. I was told I'd have to take a vacation from my job on the three days of The Change and that I would stay at a mansion, have access to the pool and good food during my stay, and that I would be safe and not have to be caged at night. I was offered the princely sum of $500 to be a wolf on three successive nights. Not a bad deal on the surface.

I asked them what else was required of me and was told that the owner of the estate just enjoyed wolves and liked seeing them roam his grounds during those nights and that paying werewolves was mutually beneficial—he could enjoy the watching and the werewolves would enjoy being pampered for two days. And the paycheck, too, of course. Heck, who wouldn't like that, werewolf or no?

I'd kept Detective Rogers in the loop each step of the way. What had happened at the mansion was technically a misdemeanor, akin to animal cruelty, and if the werewolves had been promised pay for sex that would, of course, have been pandering for prostitution. I'd so far not been offered money for sex, so the most the owner could be charged with was cruelty to animals, and perhaps pandering even if no money was involved—the law was unclear on this, unless, of course, it could be proven that the werewolves were killed on the morning after the last full moon. The police were already putting that case together.

I suggested that the police raid the estate on the morning after the first full moon and that I go undercover as a werewolf hire. Detective Rogers initially refused to let me participate, telling me that civilians couldn't be used undercover in such life-threatening situations. When I then suggested that a werewolf officer be used instead, since there were none, he arranged for a raid of the mansion for the morning after the first night and got permission from his lieutenant for me to act undercover on behalf of the police. I'd explained the layout of the estate and warned him that there would be werewolves roaming the grounds and he'd brought in the SWAD (Supernaturals, Werewolves & Demonics) Squad to our meetings.

And so, on the afternoon of the first full moon, I showed up at the estate and was taken to a cage in the garage. They'd promised me payment after the third night, which I knew would never be paid. I was given a swimsuit and offered use of the pool along with an open bar and all the noshes I could eat.

I went out and joined up with the rest of our cobbled-together pack. There were four women and another man lounging around on the patio or lazing in the pool. I gradually engaged the others in small talk, and learned that they mostly didn't recall what happened to them during The Change. Bits and pieces, yeah, but not much more. They'd been promised, as I had, food, liquor, and a nice furnished cage for the three nights. And, despite being cages, they were quite nice—material on the floor to lounge and roll around on, and the bars were padded so a caged animal couldn't hurt itself trying to escape.

The werewolves were all happy to be there, being wined and dined during the day, and thinking they'd be caged in a rather nicer cage than they had at home, with amenities and live prey to gorge on during the night and getting paid to wallow in this luxury. It was a life better than they were used to. The man was a fast-food worker, grilled the burgers and fried the fries, as was one of the women, though she usually worked the counter. One of the women said she was an actress, and though she didn't mention anything else, it was obvious she didn't work in Equity productions. The other women were office workers, low-level. People that needed the money, like the victims before them.

I brought up the idea of sex for money, and all but the actress seemed appalled. I wanted to tell them what might happen to them that night, but didn't. I rationalized that I was justified in keeping silent because even though they'd be used and abused tonight, in the end they wouldn't wind up dead like their predecessors, but that didn't calm my disgust at myself. But I'd be disgusted with myself anyway, during the night, and I'd have to find a way to live with my conscience. Sometimes, shit happens to undeserving people. I just hated being one of the people doing the shoveling.

With the evidence on the film—I assumed each of the rooms had a setup similar to the one I'd discovered the month before in the armoire—which the police would confiscate, everyone, from the host/actor to the security guards could be prosecuted, and I hoped there would be enough evidence found that the werewolves hired previously had been killed thereafter. I wanted what happened to Amanda Fuller to have just been an anomaly, but the spreadsheet I had of thirty-three victims proved it was not. But we still needed proof that the other victims had been here. Meeting these nice, everyday, normal people, werewolves all, by the pool left me sick, knowing that so many others before, just like them, had had their lives extinguished. For what? I could only imagine that the host and his guests didn't want any incriminating memory to surface, which might result in criminal charges against the participants.

We were taken to the garage and locked into our individual cages just before dark for the nearly full moon to do its magic. After The Change, three security guards, well-padded, came into the cages, one by one. My fellow werewolves snarled and lunged at them like they wanted to rip the guards to shreds, and I emulated them, feeling somewhat silly since I hadn't changed mentally that much. The guards threw down a nice steak to each of us, and while I figured it had been drugged, to go along with the scenario, I ate it and, indeed, I became dizzy. The room spun, and the next thing I knew I was grabbed, a silver collar was placed around my neck, and I was hauled out of the cage, out of the building, and up to the second floor of the main mansion. I was dragged down the corridor to the last room and put on the bed with a silver muzzle around my snout and chained to both sides of the headboard.

I won't disgust you with what happened later, with the woman who came in. It was Marjorie, I recalled, the woman from the month before, who'd had sex with the male wolf in this very room.

After enough debauchery to sate her, she curled up and fell asleep. I couldn't. I wondered if the police raid would even occur. Yes, it was cynical of me, but I wondered if the actor had enough influence in La-La Land to keep the law away from his estate, to make the police look the other way. Money does talk here. Loudly. And there have always been cops who were dirty, who could be bought. I didn't think Rogers was one of them, but who knew?

Even though I'd finished being forced to mount Marjorie close to three or so in the morning, the raid wouldn't happen until just past dawn, so that we were-wolves would have changed back to our human forms to lessen possible casualties, both police and were.

Just before dawn, a security guard came back in and unchained me, leading me, along with the others, back to the cages in the garage where we were released and allowed to Change Back at dawn.

The raid occurred that morning just after Change Back. I was first aware of it when I heard activity out on the grounds. And much, much later, when the Squad breached the garage and mansion and did a cage-by-cage search. We six werewolves, most of us again dressed, were debriefed, one by one, separately, and asked what we remembered from the night before.

Detective Rogers told me later that the others had only the vaguest of memories, knew that something happened, but couldn't really remember what. They couldn't identify anyone or remember details from after The Change. When it was explained to the werewolves what had been done to them, none of them had agreed to sex.

One of the guards turned state's evidence for a lighter sentence on the murders. Yes, most of the previous werewolves had been murdered so that anything they remembered about the night wouldn't be used to bite their sex partners or the host actor in the ass. And the film from each room was confiscated. I didn't relish the job of the officers detailed to watch them. Bad, bad porno.

I was quietly commended for my role in the investigation by the police department. Since they didn't want it known that a civilian had risked being in a potentially life-threatening police action, my role was downplayed and never made the papers. That was fine with me. I didn't want what I'd done, and especially not what I'd had to do undercover to be known. I would have even lied to the police about it, but then, they had the film.

A SECOND DEATH

by
Emily Baird

THE SECOND TIME Garnette Watters died, it was a pretty typical day for west Los Angeles. A summer breeze caressed the sidewalks, still holding just enough of the ocean's essence to mitigate the smell of car exhaust, sautéed garlic, and coffee. Overhead the sky had finally resolved to the pearly blue of an early June afternoon in the LA basin. Teens twittered and tweeted, fluttering through the crowds. Families from faraway places bonded over their hot dogs and smoothies. Couples canoodled, babies were wheeled around like royalty, toddlers skittered. All in all, it was no different from any other day at the outdoor mall where we'd been stationed since April. We'll call it The Orchard, out of deference to the nondisclosure agreements my agency and I sign with every client.

Skippy and I wandered through the clumps and clusters of people, all but unnoticed except for the occasional dog person who stopped to give Skippy some love. Skippy ate it up. Nine times out of ten, he'd roll over on his back, begging for tummy rubs. When we'd first partnered up, I'd tried to break him of the habit, but he made it clear pretty quickly that on this one issue, it was his way or the highway. He was, to put it bluntly, an unprofessional cur. If he hadn't been the most consistent scent based reanimate detector in the state—hell, probably the nation—he'd have been out on his fuzzy butt long ago. As it was, I tolerated his canine shenanigans and he allowed me to tell him what to sniff. We made a pretty good team. We'd provided our particular brand of security at all the prime tourist spots in the Southland—

rodent-run amusement parks, major concert venues, and loads of high-end malls like The Orchard.

I know what you're thinking. Don't think I haven't seen the look on people's faces when I tell them what I do. I've heard all the jokes.

"Did you drop out of the police academy or did they kick you out, mall cop?"

"Where's your Segway?"

My all-time favorite, courtesy of my former platoon leader, was "Can you detect the difference between the smell of a freshly baked Cinnabon and the smell of a Yankee Candle cinnamon roll scented candle that's been freshly lit by my ass?" Yeah. He was a sweetheart.

But what I do is serious. Deadly serious. Without me and the other members of my RAISR team—Reanimate Identification, Sanitation and Re-Mortification—there would have been no one to protect the public from the risks of inadvertent exposure to any of the myriad pathogens rattling around inside the reanimate. Besides, Yankee Candle doesn't make a cinnamon roll scented candle. They call it Cinnamon Scone.

I know what you're thinking. You're thinking, really? Are there really reanimated people walking around in shopping malls across America? Wasn't reanimating humans just a science stunt, like Dolly the Sheep or Koko, the signing gorilla?

To answer your questions: yes, sort of, and that's what the corporation that owns the patents wants you to think.

First of all, they really do walk among us, and you'd never be able to tell unless you've got a nose like Skippy.

Second, reanimates aren't all across America because it's the sort of thing that the vast majority of Americans cannot afford. And by vast majority, I mean everyone except 1% of the 1%. But that doesn't mean that people in the bottom 99% of the top 1% don't have the procedure done, especially if their entire career is based on their perky and youthful assets.

The lure of locking in the freshness is too much for a lot of actors and models, even those who hadn't quite made it into the top 1%. Far too often they'd bank on being able to maintain their earnings if they could just maintain their looks. Then those beautiful people in the bottom 99% of the 1% would have a hard time keeping up with the payments for their maintenance treatments. So, sometimes, every so often, on a very rare occasion, one of them has a system malfunction in a very public place. Like a mall. Like a high-end mall on the west side of LA.

So those high-end places employ people like me and dogs like Skippy. Skippy lets me know who's walking around dead, I keep my eye on them, and take care of things if something nasty goes down. No, not like eating brains. At least not human brains. There does seem to be some evidence that organ meat cravings go up among the reanimate, but only of species they dined on before dying. They eat plenty of produce too, don't get me wrong. But gluten? Hells no. Makes them retain fluid and they can puff up like a marshmallow in a microwave. Not pretty. I carry packs of desiccant, among other things, for just such instances.

Skippy and I wandered by three teen boys hovering around the entrance to Abercrombie and Flinch (as we'll call it, per confidentiality clauses) as though they'd been called to the mother ship. Their expressions had a certain vacancy that raised my suspicions, but Skippy gave them a pass so I shrugged it off. Then my partner had the bad form to pull on the lead as we turned toward the Dawg House. I bit back my curses when I realized that it wasn't the hot dogs that had caught his attention. Nope, Skippy was focusing the full force of his furry scrutiny on a whippet-thin redhead wrapped in sweats and dark glasses who drifted through the shadows of the awnings. Garnette Waters.

Yes, that Garnette Waters.

She was something of a regular at The Orchard. I'd seen her most of the days we'd been on this rotation. She was always sipping from a giant Living Whirld (we never signed any agreements with them) smoothie and always hiding behind a pair of huge, ridiculously expensive sunglasses. I'd never seen her wear the same pair twice. I knew they were expensive because I'd overheard her and her mother arguing about how much money she kept spending on them. Given the amounts they mentioned, either residual money was good, or they were spending way outside their means. It certainly wasn't like she'd done anything recently to get paid for.

She was alone today. That was different. I'd never seen her here without her mother. A slightly larger, blowzier version of her daughter, Emerald was clunky, chipped fiestaware in bad 70's colors while Garnette was the subtle, priceless perfection of an antique Limoges tea set—albeit in a discontinued pattern. Emerald had made a career of managing her daughter's career after her own attempts at celebrity had fallen flat. She'd carved an erratic orbit for herself through her daughter's life: pissing off producers, banging studio heads, publishing dozens of advice books on parenting (Emerald's Gem: Let them live their own lives!) and dieting (Emerald's Gem: Calories only count if you count them!) and how to feng shui your home gym or walk-in closet (Emerald's Gem: Keep weights in your purses and put them in the money quadrant!). But no matter how many waves or how much stink she made, she was nothing—absolutely nothing—without the famous name and impossibly beautiful face of her daughter.

The role that had made Garnette Waters famous had initially gone to another actress. That was common knowledge. That the actress had been Emerald Waters was not. I only knew it because I devoured online gossip sites like cotton candy—so airy, so light, so full of nothing! And because I'd overheard them so many times over these last few months. A typical conversation might go something like this:

"Another new pair? Do you even think?"

"It's bright out."

"We're not made of money, Garnette. Your treatments are eating up your royalties faster than online piracy can devour the back end."

"That's disgusting."

"No, it's not. It's business. It's money. Which you have to stop throwing around like spec scripts at a Starbucks on Sunset!"

"So why don't you get a job?"

"You take all my jobs! You and your 'youthful, natural rack.'"

"That's just silly, I haven't had a job in—how long's it been?"

"Too true, and too long."

I had never eavesdropped on them on purpose, mind you. But someone like me rarely gets noticed by someone like them. I'd learned a lot about Garnette's lack of work and Emerald's worries about money in the last few months.

Once I saw that Skippy had gotten a bead on Garnette and wasn't obsessing about Oscar Mayer, I bent to give him his praise. I even dug a treat out for him. He loves his job, but he loves him some liver treats even more. The fact that he still alerted to Garnette even though he'd seen her over a dozen times was just one more reason Skippy was the best of the best. I gave his ears a good scratching as I crooned sweet nothings into their floppy folds. I know, that's hardly standard operating procedure, but LA's not a combat zone, and as I mentioned before, Skippy comes with his own set of rules.

Out of the corner of my eye, I watched as the Abercrombie dudes realized that the hot chick they thought looked like Garnette Waters was, in fact and actuality, Garnette Waters. Their eyes got wide and they each adjusted a little something—straightening up, flexing, pulling their shirts tighter. They were only a few dozen yards away from Garnette, the breakout star of Beach Bodies, and their hormones knew it. Faster than you could minimize your screen when your mom walked in the room and then delete your browser history, the three of them whipped out their phones and completely geeked out.

"Yo! Garnette!" one of them called. "You're not working, so there's no need to tie up the girls!" He high-fived one of his buds while the third bent over laughing at his audacity.

Yes, they were talking about her breasts. For three years she'd played Laila Gibbons, the sunbathing teen forensics phenom. At some point during almost every episode her phone would ring while she was lounging somewhere in a bikini, her top untied to facilitate even tanning. Hijinks and slipping strap shenanigans would ensue as she struggled to pick up the call from the baffled beachside police agency of the week. Then she'd grab her strings, saying, "Time to tie the girls up and get down to work." It had been her breakout catch phrase. Each week she'd tie her bikini strings and get to work interviewing witnesses or taking crime scene photos or pulling things out of the dead body's pockets, or, I kid you not, performing an autopsy. In a bikini top. There'd been a poster and a calendar, dozens of subreddits and memes. Her bikini strings had even had a Twitter account.

Even as the boys looked more and more like hormonal baboons, Garnette was as smooth and classy as crème fraîche on locally sourced, organically grown heirloom berries. She smiled, and shook her head as though she hadn't heard the same joke every day for the last eight years. "The girls are strictly pay for play, boys. Unless you've got a studio contract for me, you're going to have to settle for me as is."

While Skippy and I are not technically mall security, we do occasionally intervene if the need arises. Watching the fanboys get more and more excited, and knowing Garnette's habitual desire for anonymity—and thanks to Skippy's nose, being pretty damn certain of the reason for it—this was looking like it was about to become one of those times. I straightened, gestured for Skippy to heel, and began what I hoped looked like a leisurely stroll toward the boys. I didn't even make it halfway before she exploded.

Not figuratively. Literally. In actuality. Exploded all over the goddamn place. Definitely the worst part of my job.

The water show had just started, which was really lucky for me because it meant that the tourists had gathered at the other end of the mall. It was just the boys, Garnette, me, and Skippy. The boys had been too busy with their phones to notice when the blood started streaming out of Garnette's face. The blaring notes of Sinatra from the fountains drowned out the sickening, dull, wet thud when her stomach burst.

It was a god-awful mess. Globs of tissue and dollops of offal were strewn across the entrance of Abercrombie and Fleshed. Luckily the tree cover had blocked the incident from The Orchard's live-feed webcams. Lucky for me, that is. Not so lucky for the three hormonal fanboys who'd been hanging out under said tree.

They had taken a liberal splattering of Garnette's innards. Gross? Absolutely. A guaranteed death sentence? Thanks to me and my team, probably not.

I radioed for the cleanup team and toggled my remote cell phone signal jammer even as I sprinted toward them. Dispatch garbled from my earpiece something about being only a minute or so out. I silently thanked my stars and the good planning of corporate even as I engaged with the contaminated teens.

"Whoa, what a mess, huh? I've got some cleanup folks on the way, okay?" Without the benefit of a uniform to give me authority, I used my best trainer voice to keep them focused on me and not what had just happened. Calm and even, compassionate and in charge, that was me. Teenaged boys really aren't all that different from dogs, after all.

They weren't saying much, pretty much just repeating, "Dude!" and a lot of words their mothers probably wouldn't approve of. I certainly didn't. I herded them together, gently pulled their phones from their shaking fingers while trying to direct their attention to each other and away from the ragged, inside-out bag of skin that had moments ago been a world famous—albeit washed up and reanimated—actress and swimsuit model. Even though the jammer was on, I couldn't run the risk that they'd gotten some pictures. IT would take care of cleaning the phones and making sure there hadn't been any data transfers before I toggled the jammer.

Regular mall security kept other guests away from the cordoned off area while RAISR HazMat whisked the boys into the mobile decon unit. They'd most likely be fine. None of them appeared to have any open wounds. Of course, if they'd had their mouths or eyes open during impact, that could complicate things, but we'd hold them for twenty-four to forty-eight hours in case the unlikely played out. The odds were definitely in favor of them having a great story for their frat brothers and being no worse for the wear. Heck, it wasn't out of the question that they were completely immune. Like me, almost 7% of the population was. And even for the remaining 93%, it wasn't an automatic death sentence to be exposed to the bizarre cocktail of bacterial and viral components that RipCo (RAISR's parent company) had started marketing six years ago as an 'age-defying' 'life-realignment' process.

I didn't really know how real the health threat was to the general public. Could they accidentally be 're-aligned' without being dead first? No clue. My immunity meant that I didn't have to worry about things like that. However, I'd always suspected that the company was more concerned about getting things cleaned up so that some competitor wouldn't get their hands on a sample of the goop that went into making and maintaining a reanimate. The company was so secretive about the whole process that they'd never even filed for FDA approval. All their 'life-realignments' took place in places like Sao Paolo and Manila and Bucharest.

LAPD was there in record time. I didn't know who'd called them. It sure as hell hadn't been me. Not just uniforms either. There was a plainclothes guy who waded through the mall security staff to my first barricade like they were water. Or he might have been one of the employees of Abercrombie. It wasn't out of the question that one of them had actually noticed the gruesome addition to their storefront. I made a note to find out for my final report.

Luckily my crew had been at work long enough to have removed the splat street boys and begun pathogen containment and mitigation. That was good. Safer for the public at large and easier for me to keep the scene under control. I could tell that the detective, a wiry, intense man in a surprisingly vivid blue suit, viewed things a little differently.

"Three witnesses removed? Removed where?" His voice was low, but grated like metal on concrete. "And why is a dog walker in charge of a crime scene?" There was nothing overtly intimidating about his expression, but somehow he managed to convey an anger and authority. Not enough to move me, though.

"Removed to a safe secondary location for decontamination. And the dog walker is a private contractor who acts under commission of the United States National Security Administration, Homeland Security at the express behest of the executive branch to identify, sanitize, and otherwise mitigate any and all public threats from members of the reanimate community." I smiled, trying to exude an air of polite command. My HazMat guys scurried around the thirty-foot perimeter, setting up the foam jets to stabilize the pathogens before disposal.

"Wow." He crossed his arms, tilting his head at me. He wasn't a small man, but he'd have to top six feet if he wanted to look down at me. "Some of those words were

really big. But none of them meant that you have juris-
diction over this crime scene—"

"What makes you think it's a crime scene?" I smiled
again. I've been told that my smile lacks warmth.

"What makes you think it isn't?"

"So you concede to my authority?"

"Smooth, but no." He grinned, but only with his
mouth. The kind of threat even Skippy recognized. I felt
my canine partner tense beside me and kept my frame
relaxed to reassure him. "But you were a witness, so your
account should be heard." He raised a hand toward a
couple of the uniforms milling on the perimeter. "Let me
just get someone to take your statement."

"It might have been a crime," I offered, not wanting
to deal with his minion. "More likely it was just an
accident." I nodded at my guys and they closed in on the
uniforms before they'd made it ten feet closer to the
scene. "The protocols for reanimate technology are
expensive and complicated to follow. Mistakes occur.
These things happen in the reanimate community."

He scoffed. "They're a community now?" He shook
his head, watching the foam-coated chunks of what had
once been one of *People* magazine's Sexiest Women Alive.
That had been 2005. She'd actually been alive then, given
that the first successful reanimations hadn't occurred
until 2006. "I suppose they've got lobbyists and marketing consultants working to let us know that there's
nothing to be afraid of?"

I shrugged. The politics weren't important. Reanimates were dangerous for a lot of reasons, but they were
not the cannibalistic, mindless, brain-craving killers that

the public had been expecting. We had five years of solid data proving that. Individuals lost a little something in the reanimation process, some essential, driving passion or motivation. But given the alternative, families or companies with enough resources considered that a small concession for a big gain. After the process, reanimates remained otherwise much the same as they'd been while living.

"Do you know much about the reanimate tech?" I asked.

He shook his head, all steely-eyed focus and scorn. He watched as Garnette Waters disappeared, bit by foam-coated bit, into the bio-hazard bins. "And you do?"

"That's why we're here. Handling these situations is what we do. Reanimate maintenance is tricky business, costing thousands of dollars on a regular basis, and failures are catastrophic. I've been working RAISR public interface details for the last four years. I've gotten used to seeing this kind of thing."

"So you're saying you and your dog outrank me?"

"I'm just a civilian contractor. The dog, on the other hand, does outrank you."

Skippy wagged his tail at the detective, his tongue lolling out in an obvious and desperate plea for approval. That damn dog loved him some hard cases.

"Meet Second Lieutenant Scipio Deadtracker, US Army, retired." Skippy held out a paw. The schmoozing mongrel.

The detective squinched his eyes and puckered his lips, trying to look disapproving. I wasn't buying it. Neither was Skippy, who doubled down by throwing his hindquarters enthusiastically back and forth along with his tail.

"Well hell," he finally muttered, giving Skippy's paw a gentle shake before leaning over to scratch the dog's chest. "Detective Armin Guonjian. Pleased to meet you, Lieutenant." Skippy grinned back with the pleasure of confidence rewarded. Yes, the damn dog was gloating.

"The rank's only ceremonial, but try telling him that." I caught the barest glimmer of humor in the detective's eyes as he straightened up.

"You're sure she was dead already?" He held out his hand, offering me his card with an air of challenge. His eyes were the exact same outrageous blue as his suit. Not a single, slicked-back dark hair on his head was out of place.

"A good five years or so, I'd say. Yep."

Detective Guonjian nodded. "Well, I'll just stick around for a while, until we have proof of that."

He put his hands in his pockets, turning away from me to survey the scene. Or what was left of it. I could see the side of his face pull up as he scowled at the cleanup crew. They'd finished extruding the stabilizing foam over the gore and would be done with cleanup in five to ten minutes I estimated. There were still a few bits of evidence lying around. Garnette's shoes had flown clear of her body. They lay next to two smoothie cups, which oozed orange and purple respectively. Her sunglasses, one earpiece snapped at an obscene angle and one lens popped out, floated in the brown gunk where the liquids merged.

"You think it was an accident?"

"Most likely."

"And you think your opinion matters?"

"I know it does. And when the cell jammers go offline and your cellphone buzzes to life, you'll know that too."

He scowled at me, and then pulled his phone from his pocket and scowled at it. "Jammers are —"

"Not illegal in this circumstance, per the Walker Act."

"At least until the Supreme Court rules otherwise." The phone went back in his pocket. The scowl stayed in place. "So what the hell do I call you?"

"Officially, I'm Special Agent Pamela Chapin, RAISR. Unofficially, if you ever call me Pam I will roll you up and use you to clean up after Skippy."

"And are you in charge?"

It was a trick question. He knew it. I knew it. "No. But it would thrill me to no end to be able to offer the LAPD the benefit of our resources and knowledge during what I'm sure will be a brief and very low-key investigation of this unfortunate malfunction of reanimation technology." Which meant yes. But politely.

"Okay then. What do you recommend I do next?" He crossed his arms, glaring at me even as Skippy leaned into his shins. Shepherd hair was not a nice addition to his suit.

"Identify the victim."

"How? My witnesses have been removed. The body is inside out, and rapidly being encased in foam and removed as well. You didn't coat my witnesses in that crap did you?"

"Rest assured that the government is doing everything in its power to keep citizens safe and contaminant free."

"Thanks. So who the hell was it?"

"Garnette Waters."

I watched his face. He was a pro all right. Not much more than a narrowing of his left eye to indicate how much he wanted this whole thing, and me, to go away.

"Does the press know?"

I shook my head. "No one knows —"

"Garnette!" The voice split the air, shrill and thick with panic. Detective Guonjian and I spun toward the scream. Running full tilt toward the scene was Emerald Waters. Shopping bags, receipts, and tissues littered her wake. "Garnette! My sweet baby!"

Guonjian moved quickly to intercept her before she could enter the perimeter. Appreciative of his professionalism, I flanked her.

"Ms. Waters? Emerald Waters?" he asked blandly, as he placed a comforting hand on her shoulder. The fact that he stopped her in her tracks and managed to look compassionate in the process was not lost on me. Beneath that shiny suit and pretty boy face the man had some skills.

Emerald wheeled from Guonjian to me, reeling for a fraction of an instant. It looked to me like she was trying to decide how to play the scene. "My daughter, my Garnette!" Emerald Waters cried, her fingers digging into the detective's jacket as she returned her attention to him. "Who did this to her?" She broke off, gulping air and choking out sobs.

Guonjian met my eyes over the petite woman's shaking shoulders. Who indeed.

"How?" she wailed as she caught her breath. "How did this happen? Was she shot?" The last word trailed off in a quivering whimper.

Guonjian remained unmoved by Emerald's histrionics. His veneer of compassionate professionalism never broke. He calmly patted the woman on the shoulder as he detached her from his clothes and steered her to a nearby bench.

The tourists and shoppers were long gone. A gas leak, they'd been told. Sure, it was a little hackneyed, but people never questioned it and it kept the riffraff away from the contamination threat. Gas leaks were usually too boring for the evening news to care about. It also meant that Detective Guonjian had a bit of quiet to question the victim's mother without having to leave the scene. I didn't think it was usual to question family members while men in jumpsuits cleaned up the bloody swaths of their loved one's remains, but it was becoming clear to me that Guonjian had his reasons. He probably suspected—quite correctly—that this would be his only chance to question anyone before I had the entire incident buttoned up and put to bed. He gestured for one of the uniforms to bring a bottle of San Pellegrino from an abandoned vendor cart.

I sidled closer, the unrepentant gossip fiend in me eager to hear what Emerald had been up to while Garnette's insides had cozied up to the outside. Skippy eased along with me, but then promptly lay down with a dramatic sigh. He eyed me woefully, disappointed that I seemed so distracted by human things and showed no concern about how long it had been since he'd gotten some play time. I signaled him to rest. With another sigh, he settled down, enjoying the sun and not at all interested in where Garnette Waters's mother had been.

"What makes you think your daughter was shot?" Guonjian asked after Emerald finished drinking.

She threw her hands out, fingers splayed. "All this, this…" was all she managed before breaking down again. This time the reaction seemed a little more real.

"Yes," Guonjian nodded, holding out a handkerchief. A nice one. It matched his shirt. And he was letting her get it all snotty. That was the kind of dedicated professionalism I would never have. I did happen to have a pack of tissues in one of my belt pouches, but those were for emergencies. Like pollen, or cats.

It took Emerald longer to recover from this bout. She held the handkerchief to her face for almost a full minute before finally letting her hands drop. "How could there be all this, if she hadn't been shot? Was it a bomb maybe?" She blinked her wide brown eyes at the detective. Guonjian blinked right back at her.

"Did you hear anything to make you think that?"

"No, but I wasn't here. I was at Barneys."

"So what makes you think your daughter was the victim?" Detective Guonjian indicated the taped area, grimacing the tiniest bit as he watched more of his crime scene disappear.

"The sunglasses, the smoothie cup, and those are definitely her shoes." Emerald pointed at each item in turn. "She would never just leave those laying around!"

"Her shoes?"

"They were designed just for her by Manolo. He called them bikini strings for her feet. They were her lucky shoes."

"Why weren't you with her?"

"I was paying for the sunglasses. Those sunglasses." The glasses weren't worth much now. "She'd get a new pair every day."

Guonjian nodded, as though he understood completely because, honestly, who doesn't buy a new pair of designer sunglasses everyday? "Where did you purchase the glasses?"

Emerald looked confused and glanced around as though the answer should be somewhere in front of her. Of course, being that we were still in the mall, it probably was. It was her nervously clutching hands, not her darting eyes, that came up with the answer. "Barney's." She held up the bag twisted in her fingers, staring at it. Emerald's eyes lost focus, showing her things as they had been before her daughter became foam-covered hazardous waste. "She loved Barneys. Every day, glasses and then smoothies. Always sunglasses. A lot of times she'd pick out a pair she already had. The staff at Barney's got good at making sure they rotated things for her so that didn't happen too often."

"Smoothies?" Guonjian asked, making notes on his phone.

Emerald nodded. "She loved the smoothies at Living Whirld. Life is Peachy was her favorite."

Guonjian didn't say anything, just nodded and kept tapping notes into his phone.

"That's the probiotic smoothie shop on the East end of the mall," I offered, wondering how much Guonjian really knew about the limits and protocols of reanimate tech. Not much would have been my guess. Very few people even thought the process was real, so the number who bothered to learn the ins and outs was understandably small. Minuscule really.

"Probiotic?" His head shot up, his eyes intent on Emerald's face. "You two got probiotic smoothies every day?" Apparently he knew something about it after all.

Emerald sniffed and nodded, her fingers still contorted by twists of the Barney's bag. "Every day."

His eyes flicked to me. I didn't blink, but Emerald did. Emerald's face screwed up and her mouth worked a bit, as though chewing on a really big bite of kimchi-flavored tempeh.

There was no way that Emerald Waters didn't know about her daughter's undeadness. In fact, it was pretty likely that Emerald was Garnette's conservator. Admitting that Garnette's youthful, pristine beauty had more to do with brain eating viruses and a gut full of engineered bacteria than the skill of a good plastic surgeon would do a lot of damage to Garnette's value as a brand. No one wanted a zombie telling them what perfume or shampoo to buy. I'd seen enough during my months in LA to know that there were plenty of undead in Hollywood, but no one was ever going to admit it.

"So that's what she ordered today?"

"I don't know. I was at Barney's."

"I guess it took a long time to pay for the glasses?"

Emerald colored a bit and glanced away. "There was some trouble with one of our cards."

Guonjian didn't say anything for a while, apparently fully involved with his phone. Which was cute, because it was pretty much just a snazzy notepad right now, without internet or cell reception. He looked up suddenly, and held his hand out to Emerald. "Thank you so much for answering my questions, Ms. Waters. If there's anything I or the LAPD can do for you during this difficult time, please do let us know."

She took his hand, and the card he'd so smoothly offered, with a bewildered air. Before she could fully formulate a question—much less a request for the aid Guonjian had offered—he'd handed her off to a uniform and he was striding toward the other end of the mall where a few stores were still open even though the crowds had been ushered away.

I saw what he had in mind, and Skippy roused without a word, but I still had to scramble a bit to follow. I pointed at my team second—today it was Frankie 'Frito' Lays—to let him know he was in charge as I headed off scene after Guonjian. Truth be told, I was a little thirsty and a smoothie was starting to sound good.

Guonjian was already at the counter as Skippy and I swung through the glass doors.

"Welcome to the Living Whirld, we fill life with flavor!" sang out a pink-haired girl. She never looked up from the blender jar she was rinsing out.

I moved to the counter, right behind the detective, and leaned in to read the menu over his shoulder. I was looming. It wasn't very ladylike, I know. But I'd found that looming could be very effective in getting what I wanted, when what I wanted was for someone to go away.

"Special Agent Chapin, can I get you something?" Guonjian spoke out of the side of his mouth, not bothering to turn and face me.

"Oh, I'd love a—"

"Medium Life is Berry Good, no burst!"

Yep, that was my usual. The burst thingies tended to make the smoothie a little gritty and earthy tasting.

"Hey, Mel! Looking good, farmgirl!" The young man behind the counter grinned at me, as utterly besotted as he'd been ever since I'd asked him back in April to which Baggins clan he belonged. No. That wasn't a dis on his height. He was a comfortable 5' 8", which is perfectly respectable for most girls. I asked him that because on that day, as today, his name tag proclaimed him to be, 'Bil'lbo, Whirler since 2011.' And yes, there really was an apostrophe in the middle. "And one chunk of mango for the furry dude!" Skippy woofed, then grinned like the idiot I usually think he is.

"That'd be awesome, Bil'lbo, and thanks so much for buying, Detective."

Bil'lbo's eyes got big—well, bigger—as he turned back to Guonjian. "What do you detect?" he asked, perfectly credulous. He was a sweet and gentle soul who always gave me an extra scoop of blueberries. I hoped Guonjian would take it easy on him. Bil'lbo himself had told me that he was easily disturbed by negative energy. I didn't want him to forget my blueberries.

"I was just wondering if you get many famous people in here." Subtle and roundabout were not approaches to take with Bil'lbo, but I decided to let Guonjian come to his own conclusions.

"Yes! We do!" Bil'lbo beamed at him, thrilled to be sharing this moment. Guonjian waited, phone in hand, for him to say more. Bil'lbo didn't. He just kept beaming and tossed a handful of long blond curls behind his ear. After a long 15 seconds, Guonjian finally broke down.

"Anyone interesting? Anyone I'd know?" Still too subtle, but he was getting closer.

"Yes! But I don't know if you know her." Bil'lbo waited. I watched the Guonjian's jaw clench and un-clench. It was a nicely angled jawline, but too clean-shaven for my taste.

"I might have. I meet a lot of people. Who was it?"

"Have you ever met Garnette Waters?"

Guonjian shook his head then realized that Bil'lbo need more prompting. "I have not but I'm a big fan of her work. What did she order?"

"She always gets the same thing. She comes in here, like, every morning, like right as my shift starts and is always like, thanks. She's super sweet."

"And could you tell me what her usual is?" I thought I could hear the detective's teeth grinding together a bit.

"Oh, yeah! I totally could!" Again with the pause. It'd be easy to think that Bil'lbo's sweet vacancy came with the aid of herbal assistance, but I doubted that it did. Skippy had trained as a drug sniffer back in the day, and he'd never so much as looked askance at the kid. "Oh!" Watching the light dawn in Bil'lbo's eyes must have been a daily joy and curse for a decade's worth of educators. "She always gets a Life is Peachy with no bursts. I've offered to comp her bursts before and she totally says no. Like, no effing way, no."

"And the other smoothie?" Guonjian asked. I almost felt bad for him. But Bil'lbo was helping the clock tick down, so I didn't say anything.

"Oh! Dude! You want a smoothie too? I can totally get you one! What's your pleasure?"

"Not for me. This morning. What," Guonjian broke off, turning briefly to give me a look that didn't bode well for his future enjoyment of fruity Whirld goodness. "I believe that Garnette Waters ordered TWO smoothies this morning, and it would be so helpful of you if you could tell me what they both were."

"It so totally would, wouldn't it?" Bil'bo nodded, his curls bobbing. "Oh!" Realization dawned again, a thing of beauty writ across the innocence of his brow. "But I wasn't at the counter when she came in this morning. I was helping this other lady who was trying to catch this little dog that was running around. It was like a malti-poo or a puggle, I think. Maybe it was a schnoodle. Or a havapoo. They can be very difficult."

Guonjian looked down, pinching his nose. He met my eyes again, and stuff me full of candy and hit me with a stick if it didn't look like he was laughing. "Havapoo?" he mouthed.

"Havanese poodle cross breed," I said. I couldn't help it. I actually smiled at him, and kind of meant it.

Guonjian wiped an eye and took a deep breath before looking back up at Bil'lbo's shining face. "So who was it who took Ms. Waters's order today?"

"Keifer. It was totally Keifer."

"And where's Keifer?" Guonjian leaned over to look through the tiny glass window on the one door behind the counter.

Bil'lbo's eyes got wide. "You're totally right! She's in the back. Dude! You're like that psychic detective guy on TV!"

"Thanks so much. Could you please ask her to step out here for a moment?"

"Oh, totally! Keifer! Keifer! There's a detective dude out here who wants to ask you about your smoothies!"

The door swung open, pushed by the narrow back of a young woman in a too-tight Living Whirld T-shirt. Her pink hair spiked from her head in random clumps, a giant plastic tub of 'Living Whirld Probiotic Burst' in her arms.

"God, Bill, how many times do I have to tell you, it's Kefir. Like the yogurt drink, not the drunk actor."

Bil'lbo muttered a quick apology and then resigned himself to making sidelong glances at me while he threw ingredients into the air and caught them with his blender jar.

Kefir—seriously, it was on her nametag—put her hands on the counter, staring as hostilely at Guonjian as a woman named for a yogurt drink can. "I've got eighty gallons of guava nectar to unload and then I am outey, so let's get to it."

"You helped Garnette Waters about 15 minutes ago?"

Kefir nodded. "She ordered a Life is Peachy, no burst for herself and a bursting Life is a Bowl of Cherries, probably for that older lady she's usually with. Didn't see her today. Which was cool, because that chick never tips. Boobsalicious, on her own? She left a ten dollar tip. Which totally made me reevaluate my world view." She reached out to tap the tip jar—a hollowed out coconut—and grinned. She had a small tattoo on the inside of her wrist. A butterfly, formed from four scrolled letters intertwined. YOLO. I wondered if Guonjian recognized it.

"And that's what you made? One with a burst and one without? Or did you decide to give both smoothies a burst of life?" I had hoped he wouldn't ask that question. It was looking like he did know what those four letters meant. They didn't refer to the played out Instagram meme, although that made a nice cover story when people saw their tats. Nope. My guess was that smoothie girl here was a card-carrying member of YOLO: You Oughta Live Once, only the most subversive and radical anti-reanimate group on the west coast.

"What's the big deal? Did some re-annie steal her sippy cup and go kablooey all over?"

"Something like that. Nice tat, by the way." Damn. He was totally onto it.

"Thanks! My friend has a private studio in Venice and I saw this in his sketch book. I totally had to beg him for it, but it's just beyond, isn't it?" She held her arm out for better viewing, admiring the art. "Wait. What?

Someone really did blow up out there?" Her face registered genuine shock. "Oh my God! That really happens? I mean it's in all our training videos and we have to read these legalese warnings before taking the job, but seriously? I thought it was just hyper—what do you call it? Hyper-bowl? To keep us from giving out extra bursts so they could save money."

"Nope, not hyperbole," Guonjian told her. "Did you use the same blender for both smoothies? Without rinsing maybe?"

Kefir shook her head. "We never do that. But I didn't make the order. Bil'lbo started on it while I was ringing her up. She kept pulling out bills and coins and we kept adding them up. Took forever to get to $9.79. And then she found that ten in her pocket and just threw it in the coconut. Which was totally awesome of her, right?"

"Totally. Thanks for your help." He held out his hand to her, but his eyes were already following Bil'lbo. Bil'lbo saw us watching and flipped the blender jar into the air before catching it, unlatching the lid and pouring the contents into a cup.

"I threw in a little something extra for you," he told us, leaning in conspiratorially. "Extra blueberries, and a burst of life on the house!"

I took my smoothie with a smile, palming the proffered mango chunk. "Thanks Bil'lbo. I bet that's how you treat all the girls."

"Only the pretty ones like you, Mel." He really was a sweet soul. A sweet, simple soul. I took a sip and did my best to smile back at him. Damn, I hated a gritty smoothie.

"What about those training videos Kefir here was talking about? Aren't you afraid of giving out the wrong thing to the wrong person?" Guonjian couldn't quite let it drop. I didn't see how it mattered. It's not like Bil'lbo meant for anyone to get hurt.

"What could be wrong about blending up organic, sustainably farmed fruit from the earth and healing, life-enhancing probiotics?" Bil'lbo peered intently at Guonjian, as though his answer meant the world to him.

Guonjian shrugged. "It kinda sucks for the fruit." He nodded at Kefir and headed out the door.

I followed. Skippy gave me mournful looks as we walked back into the sunshine. He sniffed suggestively at the fruit in my pocket. He knew he wasn't getting the mango. I never gave him things from civvies. I'd take their offerings and then switch it for one of Skippy's usual treats. I was too focused on Guonjian at the moment to pull a substitute out. Skippy had no patience for it. He nosed my hand as I hurried after the detective.

"So that's it, right?" I asked, skipping a bit to keep up with him as he strode toward the parking structure. "Just an accident?"

Guonjian shrugged. "Doesn't really matter anyway. This just showed up in my inbox." He held up his phone, a copy of Garnette Waters's death certificate on the screen. It was dated May, 2007 from Sao Paulo, Brazil. Cause of death? Accidental overdose. My guess was she'd overdosed on a unique viral and bacterial cocktail prepared for her at the bargain price of four to five hundred thousand dollars, and that it hadn't been an accident at all.

Either way, it didn't matter. With a death certificate already on file, there was no way that the LA DA would be able to file charges. That meant there was no reason for Guonjian to stick around.

"Didn't you expect this?" I asked.

Guonjian shrugged, tucking his phone away. "I suppose I did. But I wouldn't do what I do if I was the sort of person who could just walk away from something so obviously wrong."

"But now?"

"Now, I have to. Maybe next time, I won't. Maybe someone will change the law. Just because someone's already dead doesn't mean they can't be murdered."

I hadn't thought of it that way before. But Garnette had probably just taken a sip of the wrong smoothie. Or maybe Bil'lbo had been too generous. The whole thing was probably just a sad, horrible mistake.

"Well, it's been great," I offered, lamely. I think I'd enjoyed watching him do his job more than I wanted to admit. It certainly was a hell of a lot more interesting than telling tourists where the webcams were so they could wave to their friends at home, or trying to explain why a celebrity chef would insult every patron who walked through his door by calling his restaurant The Fat Pig.

"I appreciate your cooperation, Special Agent Chapin." He had only taken a step or two before he turned back. I was a little embarrassed that he caught me still watching him. "Can I call you Mel?"

"Sure," I nodded. "Feel free to call me, if you've ever got any questions that I could help with, I mean."

He smiled. "Enjoy your smoothie, Mel."

I held it up in salute and then forced myself to turn around and head to Third Street rather than watch him walk away. He'd been more tenacious than any of the other cops I'd encountered during incidents like this. He'd actually asked questions, looked for answers. That hadn't happened before. Not a lot of people cared about the reanimate, if they thought about them at all. I wondered who he'd known, what he'd been through, that made him ask those questions even though he had to have known that he'd never have a chance to bring charges against anyone for Garnette's re-death.

In the last five years, over the five continents of human habitation, not once had there been one crime, one murder, one rape, one injustice perpetrated by a reanimate. It just wasn't in them anymore. I couldn't help picturing Garnette as I'd seen her last: as perfect and as pristine as porcelain, standing beneath a canopy of jacaranda blossoms. Unchanged and unchanging, rendered into nothingness by the need to remain desirable. Those purple flowers all around her had been just as beautiful as she, but somehow more meaningful. Pushed from the tree by nature's need to move forward, pulled to the ground by the universe's inexorable progress toward a conclusion both unknown and inevitable, those flowers were part of it all. But Garnette had been removed from the natural order, denied her place in the universe. She'd been turned into something that would never come to full fruition, something hollow and simple. Maybe it had been her choice. Maybe she'd known it wasn't safe when she'd taken that last big swig of smoothie.

Maybe not.

Traffic was quiet for the time of day. It probably hadn't picked up yet after the 'gas leak' had forced so many closures. It wouldn't be long, I knew, before the street filled up again with drivers hunting in vain for a parking spot and bemused pedestrians, intent on their busy days. Even as I watched, a sporty little convertible pulled up and paused in the red, blinkers on. An athletic figure broke from the cover of a building and vaulted into the car, not bothering with silly things like doors or opening. His blond hair rippled in the wind as the car pulled away, the red-haired driver laughing at his exuberance.

I couldn't laugh though. I suppose it didn't really surprise me that Bil'lbo and Emerald should know each other. He'd been serving her smoothies every day for months. What had surprised me, other than just seeing the two of them together, had been what I'd seen as his hair had blown back in the LA afternoon air. The scrolling script of a four-lettered tattoo which flowered across the back of his neck. Just four letters. But they said more than I wanted to know.

Not that there was anything either I, or the law, could do about it now.

"Come on, Skippy, our shift is over."

Skippy shook himself, sneezed, and followed me back.

THE SEER
AND THE SEEN

by
Lynn Finger

As I CROUCHED at the console where chief space station engineer Lt. Myers had met his end, I stretched out my hand, with my sensing device at the ready. I had come out during sleeping hours—when the lights were off—because I love the silence and I can concentrate better. I wasn't sure if it was light or dark, but I didn't care about the darkness. I am one of those rarities. Not many of us exist really; I'm a genetic mutant. That's fine with me, go ahead and recoil, I'm used to it. I can feel the drawing back, I can hear the forced laugh when I meet folks and they notice I'm different in a way that repels them. It doesn't matter what planet they're from. They're thinking, in this perfect universe, why was I allowed to grow up this way? I grew up without eyes. "Otherwise normal," the geneticists said. Apparently the genetic engineer overseeing my fetal development fell asleep at the volumetric flask, so to speak. But it doesn't matter to me. I'm not even a minority. There's not many of me around. I'm a mutant.

Sorry, let me introduce myself. I am Sofia Goodreck, galactic private investigator. In all other ways normal. But blind. And of course what does the blind freak—moi—do with my life? Become a detective, of course. There's probably a lot of psychological compensation in that professional move, but that's really other people's problem, not mine. I became the seer, as I look for the unseen.

So just to let you know, at 2:00 am inside this little work cubicle, in a space station orbiting near HIP 13044 (a planet outside the Milky Way, where I normally live), I really wasn't feeling excited about this investigation. I'd been informed that a high level engineer had been killed in this area and it obviously wasn't an accident. No one wanted to say "murder" just like no one liked to say "blind." It was so untidy and not very progressive sounding.

Lt. Myers had died from a surgical laser cut to the throat while he sat at his console. There was little blood and few clues left at the scene. The way I figured it, the engineer possibly had been imbibing or high on something, flipped the wrong switch and just got in the way of the laser, which is supposed to be used as a surgically precise cutting instrument for tools and experiments. The only thing that didn't jibe with my theory was the whole "ghost" thing.

"His last report to us was that it was, well, a ghostly figure," the captain had stated to me, embarrassment in his voice. "We don't know what the anomalous signal was, whether a ghost, or alien life form, or what. We've hired you to find out what the damn thing is, we don't want it on our station, and we would like you to see if it killed Lt. Myers." At the word "see" he'd immediately fumbled and backed down. "No, I didn't mean 'see', I meant—"

I'd decided to put him out of his misery, and interrupted smoothly, "Don't worry, Captain, I believe I can help you out, and I know what you meant." The captain had a faint odor of sweat and vodka—not an offensive combination, but he was oozing stress, and I was beginning to get jittery myself.

We'd settled ourselves in an area that I presumed the captain felt was comfortable, although there was little cool airflow and my seat was lumpy. I had, however experienced worse, so I didn't mention it. We were in a private room, away from the business of keeping the space station operating and the staff required to do this. The footsteps had faded away and voices had become muffled, yet the captain still had not seemed at ease. He'd crossed and uncrossed his legs, adjusting himself, which had caused creaking sounds from his seating and crinkling from the fabric of his jumpsuit. His level of alertness had seemed extreme, to me, as if he thought he might be the next target of the murderer.

"Tell me what happened," I'd said.

"Lt. Myers was one of our best engineers. He was unflappable, calm, professional, and the guy was a genius. We were glad to have him here. But..." I'd heard more fidgeting, adjusting. "But right before he was killed, he started losing his edge."

"In what way?" I'd asked.

"He started talking about seeing some ghost readings, unexplained energy patterns on the screens. And Myers wasn't one for loose ends. He liked explanations, and that's why we liked him as the ship's chief engineer."

"So when did he start talking about ghosts?" I'd said. "And what did he mean?"

"He started up on this ghost talk two months ago. He came to me in private at first. Worried about these elusive readings he was getting. He wasn't sure what was causing them and was concerned for the safety of all of us on the space station. As it turns out, his own safety was in jeopardy."

"Were there any other theories about what was going on?"

"Yes, a few," the captain had said. "Rumors started spreading. Myers became jumpy when he was with the other crew. He mentioned the ghost readings and seemed nervous as he went through his day, and you know how folks will talk."

"Yes, I do."

"They were calling him crazy, too much time in space, too much time at the same job, losing his touch. It's true, he wasn't himself."

"But what was the explanation for these ghost readings?" I'd persisted. "Even if he was losing his edge, the readings did appear on the scanners, from the information you provided me. They were real."

The captain had paused and said, "Why don't you listen to the last recordings we have of these ghost readings right before Myers was killed?"

Good, some real evidence. So far all I had heard was that an engineer, used to perfection and always being right, had met up with a reading he couldn't explain and become unhinged.

The captain had placed something on the table in front of me, with a click. "Listen," he'd said.

The first words were, "Oh God, not again," said in a whisper.

"That's Lt. Myers," the captain had added.

Then Myers's voice changed to a professional tone as he commented, "This is an unfamiliar, unidentified reading." His voice trembled. "It is an energy detection that appears and then disappears off the screens, then reappears elsewhere in the station. This isn't possible!" he exploded before maintaining calm again. "This is the ghost reading, Captain, I was telling you about. The console is not malfunctioning. These are not released gases out of some of the living quarters that didn't get expelled properly. I've checked the air composition in the passages of the space station." His voice disappeared again into a whisper as he appeared to talk to himself. "What is it, what is it? Oh God no!" There was a quick series of sounds like he was frantically keyboarding information into his system, or maybe reaching for a weapon? Then everything fell silent until the sound of a body falling to the floor. The audio had clicked off.

I'd sat, thinking. The emotion was real. But were the readings real? "Did anyone else get a chance to examine these records?"

"Yes," the captain had said. "Yes, we did examine the records, and they defy explanation at present. We were able to identify some molecular similarities between the different images. They appear to be some form of gas, but nothing familiar to us. We don't know what they are. No one else in the station detected them or saw them. Only Myers. Right now, all we know is that these molecular manifestations can disappear and reappear. Like a ghost."

"Thank you, Captain. Can you show me to my quarters now?"

I sat on a nice, soft cushion in the small quarters where they had put me, but small was good, because I didn't need space to think, and being myself, I liked not having to count too many steps between walls.

My mind was busy with the information I'd been given. A sneaky molecular grouping that came and went inhabited the station. It scared Myers and was present when he died, although I couldn't see how it could have caused his death. Molecules were tricky things, as I knew so well. I was the Private "I" without the Eyes. It took only one flip of the genetic switch to make a mouse into an elephant, and an otherwise normal baby into a blind mutant.

I'm not saying Myers didn't know what he didn't know. But I wondered who had thrown the switch on this ghost reading, and what it would take to bring it to light. Sometimes when we hear sounds in the hallway, they can sound like a monster's footsteps, but when someone finally goes to check, it's just the cat.

I was definitely on the side of the cat theory. This is why. Some years ago, I had been involved with a murder case that seemed to have no earthly explanation. It had also taken place on a space station. The victim's blood had been drained. The inhabitants were split between blaming all sorts of scary things that go bump in the night, including vampires, werewolves, witches, zombies, and some other creatures. The sky was the limit. I've never seen any of these creatures, but I know what it is like to feel like one. After some investigation, as it turned out, no monster was involved, just a mutant—like me!—whose genetic makeup had predisposed him to eating blood. Hey, it happens. He tried to hide it, and who could blame him? But finally he was overcome with hunger. There's only so much beef tartare available in space.

When he was arrested, I didn't get a chance to talk to him about how he was born. I just wondered if we were next to each other's flasks as baby cells, and whether we could blame the same thoughtless genetic engineer who messed me up. But that was years ago.

I knew if I could explain the molecular grouping that Myers saw, that we would get the answer to the murder. Everyone was focused in the wrong direction. They were trying to explain Myers, why he had changed, gotten strange, lost his edge, whether or not he'd killed himself. I wanted to explain the ghostly reading. Once that was understood, we would have the answer. I wasn't able to sleep, so I took another trip to the murder scene.

I stretched my hand-held sensor to the area where the engineer had fallen—a simple, routine operation at this point. I was attempting to collect information regarding DNA, skin cells, time of death, temperatures in the area, and other data that I could "look" at. I wanted this investigation to be routine. I didn't want any weirdness, although the final report of Myers to the captain was, let's face it, weird.

After scanning the console and the engineer's chair, I moved to the floor.

And then I heard it. And felt it.

Although I'm not prone to fear, again another defense mechanism of mine to prove I'm more courageous than other folks ("Look at the blind girl kick your ass!"), I felt the hairs prick up on my arm and neck in an unpleasant way. I heard a shuffling sound, and then the room turned cold.

Maybe all the lights went out. I wouldn't know, but that would be the next thing to happen, right? I'm acquainted with ghost stories.

Ghost stories are things fearful people tell each other over flickering bonfires, in old primitive outdoor meadows, surrounded by the edges of the scary forest where noises can sound like really large monsters coming to eat them. Locked into that tiny circle of light around the fire, staring at the flames for courage, backs turned to the black night, telling ghost stories somehow keeps ghosts away. Like some kind of magic spell.

I don't believe in ghosts. But there was something definitely odd about the drop in room temperature, the weird shuffling sounds—not standard issue footwear—and my hackles rose. I wanted to yell out, "Back off!" but I was so scared that I couldn't move.

After a moment, I forced myself to slowly stand. I thought I could feel a breeze, but nothing definite. I wondered if I would be decapitated too, like Myers, but forced myself not to duck down defensively.

"Who is it?" I finally asked, addressing myself to the shuffling in the silence.

A voice intruded into my thoughts. "They think I'm a ghost," the voice whispered to me. "Only in their instruments, though. I'm as real as you are."

Was I being set up? I admit I have a suspicious mind. It could have been a joke, or a test to see just how gullible I was. But the captain certainly seemed to think there was a "something," a ghost or other unexplained event, messing up the ship's instruments and jacking up people's fear levels. Maybe even causing murders.

"Okay," I said, "So you're not a ghost. Who or what are you?"

"I'm Ria. I need your help," she whispered. "I'm caught in a molecular exchange. But I'm as real as you are. I am real."

Real? Not quite. I didn't want to listen to this cold voice, this Ria, tell her story. But it was part of the job. People—er—people and ghosts, it seems—would take as long as they needed to tell their story before getting to the point. I really didn't know what I was dealing with here, but I didn't want to listen to this female voice insist she was "real." Like me insisting I can see. It doesn't work that way.

I decided to cut to the chase. "Did you kill Myers?"

"No, I didn't kill Myers!" was the abrupt reply. "You're supposed to be smart."

I ignored this dig from this unknown entity. "But you were there," I said.

"You need to help me," she repeated in a whisper. "You're a mutant. You would understand. I'm a mutant too."

"Okay, I'll bite," I said. "What kind of mutant?" I admit I was tired and was looking forward to returning to bed, and the ghost wasn't helping me. The novelty had worn off, and unless the ghost could give me some good information, I wasn't interested in talking to the mutant. Mutant ghost.

"It happened when I was a child. Ten years ago. I was eight. We were transporting molecularly—taking a trip with family. Due to some chromosomal malformation of mine, I was unable to come back to complete bodily re-assemblage, as they say. Due to my not being whole at the start. So I got trapped in this lighter-than-air place — like a gas. But I'm not a gas," Ria stated.

I had heard about some of these transport dissolutions. They were rare, but had happened in the past. "Look," I said. "I'm really sorry. But do you have any information for me about the murder? You were there, right?"

"I was trying to warn him," the mutant said, "because—" then suddenly shifting gears, "why should I help you?" she demanded.

"So we can find the killer? So no one else will be harmed?" Did sarcasm work on gases?

The voice scoffed. "No one else will be harmed. This was a one-time thing."

"How do you know?" I asked. Was I really interrogating an energetic collection of molecular disarray?

"He made enemies," Ria said. "He was the only one they hated."

"What enemies?" I said.

"You have to promise to help me first," Ria said in her silvery whisper. "If you can help me with my reassembly, you know, make me back into a body, I can help you solve this."

"You haven't shown me you have any other information. Besides, I don't know if I can help you. I wouldn't know where to start."

There was a pause. More shuffling. A whispered, "I'll think about it." And Ria was gone.

THE NEXT MORNING I woke up late. I pulled on my jumpsuit, tied back my hair, and ran to the meeting room on the far deck of the ship to interrogate the rest of the staff. Although I'm blind, I'm pretty good at picking up on emotions like fear, nervousness, anger. I have a good sense of smell, and when people's voices change, or they get agitated, or suddenly work up a sweat, I can build on that information.

But the ghost had said this was a one-time deal. If the ghost was right, this could be a revenge killing, either over money or love. Something that was specific to Myers. Someone he loved or had betrayed.

After ten hours of drinking freeze-dried coffee, smelling/sensing/deducting, and quite a few lame blind jokes (you'd be surprised at what people might blurt out when embarrassed), my work was rewarded. Out of all the scientists, engineers, maintenance staff, etc., it had finally come down to just one person.

This person was Dr. Shey. He was irritable and bossy, sounded like an older, upper-ranked person, and he didn't answer questions directly. He also fidgeted. Throughout the interview, he acted bored and in a hurry to go. Dr. Shey didn't laugh at my blind jokes and seemed dismissive of the process.

He challenged me. "How do you know Myers didn't off himself? It's not a big deal to aim a laser in the wrong direction, and he didn't have a lot of friends. He should have been transferred off onto the nearest space hub, anyway."

"So what would be his motive for doing so?" I asked.

"The motive would be self loathing since no one liked him anyway."

"That's not enough. Lots of people don't like themselves. He would need more, like a huge loss, financial ruin, professional ruin, loss of a loved one, but none of those have happened. In fact, he seemed pretty lucky."

I said that on purpose. The guy hadn't been lucky. From what Shey had told me—he claimed Myers had stolen one of his research ideas—Myers had been Machiavellian. But I was hoping to gain more information by pushing some buttons.

"Lucky!" he exploded. "He wasn't lucky, he was a liar!" Catching himself, he clamped down on his words.

If Myers had stolen Shey's idea, Shey had a direct motive for killing him. However, after Shey had finished giving his side of the story, I found myself not liking Myers very much, either. Not that Myers had needed to be bumped off. But I could see there might be some anger directed his way, and on a space station this small, only 300 hands, there was nowhere to go.

"I was working on molecularly unstable forms of energy," Shey said. "Things that had a different vibrational rate than anything we have seen before, including solids, liquids, and gases. I discovered this while I was studying a life form we found on one of our study planets. It really was quite unique. It was like a starfish—small, no spine—but it could change into a gas and then completely return to its solid form. We discovered this when we confined them to an aquarium in the lab.

"Of course, this was very exciting stuff, to find something that could change forms like this. And Myers said he could lend his knowledge of life form detection." Dr. Shey gave a bitter laugh. "Yeah, right. Before I knew it, he'd put his name on the research I had spent years on, and gave this transformation a name: the Myers Transition."

I couldn't say that I had heard of it. But it sounded important.

"We used to be friends. Can you imagine that I used to trust that scumbag? Have you ever met someone with no redeeming qualities at all?" he asked.

"Yes, unfortunately," I said. "Would you say Myers was someone the world would be better off without?"

"No, never. I just wanted him off the ship, bon voyage and toujours gai, as they say."

"But he stole your research," I said.

Another bitter laugh. "Yes, that he did, although not much good it does him now."

"So what happened with the research after that?" I asked.

"Well, I still have my notes and results. The research was mine whether he put his name on it or not."

"Did you ever find a way to control the starfish changes?" I asked.

"Yes—we were working on some methods to get the starfish to change into a gas and back. They seemed to respond to differing frequencies of light. The light would stimulate their molecules to reshape them. We had developed a method to cause this transition."

"But if it was a gas, couldn't it get out of the aquarium?" I asked.

"That was the surprising thing," Dr. Shey said. "They could get out, because they would vaporize through the screens on top, so then we sealed the aquarium. We found that these gases could physically manipulate the lids on their tanks and even make slight sounds. This made the research even more exciting, and then we realized that these creatures weren't really gases, but, for lack of a better term, a solid that was 'molecularly unstable.' They had some properties of a solid, such as form, ability to move objects, and to vocalize, but with the properties of gases like diffusing into areas and in some instances being undetectable."

That term "molecularly unstable" sparked something in my mind. Ria had said that when she was taking her trip with her family, she had experienced molecular disarray. Like these starfish.

"A solid that is molecularly unstable—you mean like the 'ghost'?" I asked.

Dr. Shey laughed again, his laugh sharp. "Oh yeah, the ghost." He snorted. "Myers used to mention this ghost reading on the instruments. Crazy. Can you imagine?"

I sat silent for a moment. I had run into the ghost and heard the last transmission to the captain from Myers. But Shey might have been willing to say anything to discredit this guy.

"Did you know what he was talking about?" I asked.

Another laugh. "I don't have to. The guy was nuts."

"The captain mentioned the ghost to me," I said. "He didn't seem to think it was crazy."

Another snort from Dr. Shey. "People can be afraid of their own shadows if you start the right rumor. There was nothing there. He probably killed himself, plain and simple."

"Did you start the rumor?" I asked. "Did you start telling others that Myers was losing it to discredit him?" I said.

"What? No!"

"But you learned how to manipulate energy. You could have used one of the starfish gases to trigger the laser without even being in the room."

"We'd had some successes with that transition, but no one believed his ghost stories!" Dr. Shey's voice was rising.

"You hated him and still hate him," I said. "He betrayed you. And now that he's gone, the research is yours and yours alone. You have motivation and you had the means, by your own report. Now that he is dead, you have your work back, and he's no longer able to steal anything else from you, including your ideas or your trust."

"You think I killed him?" Dr. Shey demanded.

"I think you had motive and means," I said. "And I'm taking you into custody."

I called for security. Dr. Shey screamed all the way down the passageway, until I could no longer hear, that he was innocent and had done nothing wrong. I'm glad I was unable to see the spectacle.

After all the yelling and drama, I retreated back to my small, private quarters. It felt like a haven after talking to Dr. Shey. He really was the only suspect that made sense. He truly hated Myers and was glad he was gone. He had a way to manipulate forms with his starfish that could turn into something less than a solid.

But there was still a thought nagging at me. Ria had been there when Myers died. For someone molecularly disassembled, she had a lot of knowledge about the motive. She said he had enemies. She knew that he alone was the target, out of everyone on the ship. Was she an accomplice? And if Shey's research were true, then would she be able to manipulate things too, just like the starfish in Myers's and Shey's research? And in the old ghost stories, the poltergeists were said to toss things across the room. Might Ria, too, have been able to turn the aim of the laser? But Shey had a clear motive for killing Lt. Myers. Ria had been present at the scene, but what possible motive might she have had?

I don't believe in ghost stories, but I do believe in things I cannot see. I knew from past experience that mutants might be deficient in some areas, but could do really well in others. I was possibly taking a chance, but I went to the brig to ask Dr. Shey a few more questions, particularly about his invention that could turn the starfish back to solid form.

Later that night, I returned to the scene of the crime, the engineering center where Myers had met his end. It was really the middle of the night, so still and silent you could hear a pressurized suit decompress. I was there for a reason. I thought I had my answer, but I wasn't completely sure. I had a ghost to interrogate, and let's just say I had an ace up my sleeve. I didn't have to wait long, for immediately the temperature dropped a bit, a cold breeze seemed to waft by, and I heard the whisper, "Can you help me?"

"Yes, Ria, I think I can," I replied calmly. "Even though you weren't helpful to me about the murder."

"I don't have any information," she said. "I thought you were supposed to be smart."

Even though she had dematerialized years ago, she still sounded like the eight-year-old she had been at the time.

"Yes, I believe I can help you, Ria," I said, "but I need to tell you something."

"Yes," the ghost breathed.

"I know why you killed Myers."

There was a silence, deeper than before. Like breath being held, if there had been any. "Didn't kill him," she snapped. "You're supposed to be—"

"Yeah, yeah, I'm supposed to be smart. But I know why you killed him. He had the power to help you, but he refused because even though he had experimented on starfish, he thought if he assisted you in assembling yourself it would further disrupt the energies within the ship and possibly destroy many lives." Again, I just made up that last stuff about Myers fearing that he would destroy lives. You never know what people might blurt out when they think you've misjudged the situation.

"That is not why!" Ria snapped, rage electrifying the air. "We were in love, and he was supposed to make me back into human form so we could be together! I loved being near him. He made me feel real. He talked about how when he made me human again, we would never be apart. He was sweet to me. He said he loved me. And he was a liar! He wanted me to disappear, so I made him disappear," she hissed. "He didn't know I could manipulate the instruments," she added smugly. "He thought he knew everything. He didn't know I could fool the instruments and keep him from knowing where I was. But I made him disappear. And I can make you disappear too, you blind-as-a-bat idiot!"

Honestly, I wished her level of insults would improve. I didn't have the heart to tell Ria that Myers had simply been using her, studying her from a scientific viewpoint, and needed her to go along. He used the oldest trick in the book.

But I didn't have time to feel for Ria. I was poised for her next movement as the air wavered around me, shifting, changing. I had memorized the room layout and knew where the laser was. I experienced right then, perhaps, some of the same terror that Myers had felt the night he died. But I fought it back, and then I used my ace.

My ace was Dr. Shey, who had recently been released into my custody. Dr. Shey was at the ready, waiting for my signal. I fell to the floor as the ghost moved to electronically trigger the laser again to kill me. Dr. Shey moved forward and switched his new invention, radiant with light at different wavelengths, into the ghost.

Her molecules were set into motion and she reformed herself, screaming at the top of her lungs as she fell to the floor by me with a thud. Whatever her chromosomal malformation was, it didn't involve her vocal chords.

Dr. Shey said, "It worked!"

I stayed low, grabbing Ria's hands to apply the automatic wristlock, while I heard Dr. Shey throw his lab coat to modestly cover her new molecular structure.

"How did you know?" she cried. "How did you know?"

"I wasn't really sure until your complete confession," I said, "but the ship's instruments put you at the scene of the crime, and you had the most motivation of anyone, since you wanted so badly to be re-assembled, to be human again."

"Can you blame me?" she cried.

"You'll never be fully human," I said. "You're a mutant like me."

I turned to the direction of her voice. "You're under arrest through the Agency of the Federation of Space Stations and Molecularly Unstable Entities," I said.

"Molecularly unstable—what?" she cried.

"Yes, I did my homework," I said, "and I advise you to remain silent. Even molecularly unstable entities have rights here."

She fell silent. By that time, the security staff had arrived. They came forward and took her away.

On my way home on the shuttle, I reflected on how neatly this had worked out. A murder was solved, a gaseous person had become solid again, Dr. Shey had his research back and would be vindicated soon, and the space station was de-ghosted, so to speak.

The captain was pretty pleased. He gave me a bonus and said I was always welcome back, which I liked. Even Dr. Shey agreed.

I may not be super smart, but let's just say I'm smart like a blind fox. This is galactic investigator Sofia Goodreck signing off.

CONTRIBUTORS

Helen Angove began her working life as an electrical engineer on the south coast of England, and then worked briefly as a pricing analyst for an electricity supply company. After this she trained to be a priest in the Church of England, and spent seven years in full time ministry before deciding that she had to leave before she tore out *all* her hair. Now she is living with her husband and two children in Southern California, and, against all the dictates of common sense, pursuing a career in writing. Visit her at http://www.helenangove.com.

Old enough to know better, **Leonhard August** is just starting a fiction writing career. He has had parallel careers in technology R&D, and management of start-up ventures based on new tech. Len has several technical publications to his credit and has taught computing related subjects at the community college level. Len has spent the last 20 years working with Native American people through economic development programs. Most recently, he has been active in the implementation of community development organizations, CDFIs and credit unions. He lives in the Southwest to facilitate access to his fabulous grandchildren. Visit him at http://leonhardaugust.wordpress.com.

Typical of most writers, **Emily Baird** is over educated and under employed. Although subject to occasional bouts of retail therapy, Emily prefers to avoid malls, even when they aren't riddled with the undead. Check out her first Elm Books story in *Death on a Cold Night*.

Cover artist **Virginia Cantarella** is a nationally known medical illustrator, painter, and book designer. She has illustrated over 20 major medical texts; has written, illustrated, and formatted two books of her own to be nationally released next year by Elm Books; and illustrated and formatted numerous other books—several cookbooks, a book on golfing, and a book on phonics. She is a fine arts painter as well, doing landscapes, still life paintings, and exhibiting regularly. Her work can be seen at http://www.virginiacantarella.com.

H. Tucker Cobey is a writer and a professional SAT instructor. A black belt in Tae Kwon Do, he is also fully qualified to operate 17th century field artillery.

As **Charlie Cochrane** couldn't be trusted to do any of her jobs of choice—like managing a rugby team—she writes, with titles published by Carina, Samhain, MLR and Cheyenne.

Charlie's *Cambridge Fellows* series of Edwardian romantic mysteries was instrumental in her being named Author of the Year 2009 by the review site Speak Its Name. She's a member of the Romantic Novelists' Association, Mystery People, International Thriller Writers Inc and is on the organizing team for UK Meet for readers/writers of GLBT fiction. She regularly appears with The Deadly Dames. Visit her at http://www.charliecochrane.co.uk.

Jess Faraday, mystery editor for Elm books, is the author of several novels, including the Lambda-shortlisted *Affair of the Porcelain Dog* and the steampunk thriller *The Left Hand of Justice*. She can be found at http://www.jessfaraday.com.

Lynn Finger likes to consider the Big Questions through a science fiction lens. A violist and Yoga practitioner, she's also an avid reader and writer of poetry.

Gay Toltl Kinman has nine award nominations for her writing; short stories in American and English magazines and anthologies; several children's books; a Y.A. gothic novel; six adult mysteries; several short plays produced; articles in professional journals and newspapers; and she has co-edited two non-fiction books. Kinman has library and law degrees. Visit her at http://www.gaykinman.com.

Mark Hague, author and artist, lives in sunny (and occasionally very hot) Southern California, and when he's not at his computer writing (or playing solitaire!) or making Artist Trading Cards (ATCs) to swap with other artists, his nose is buried in a mystery book. A political junkie in a past incarnation, he loves dogs, but isn't presently owned by one.

Angelia Sparrow is a prolific author of dozens of novels and short stories. She is best known as an author of GLBT romance. She writes in a variety of genres, including horror, paranormal, fantasy and science fiction. She is a former library paraprofessional who traded her card catalogue for ten in the wind and the hum of the highway. She works steadily on the newest pieces, haring off on tangents as the muses move her. Visit her at http://www.brooksandsparrow.com.

CPSIA information can be obtained
at www.ICGtesting.com
Printed in the USA
FSOW01n2239060616
21231FS

9 780988 611672